Lotta's Progress

LOTTA'S PROGRESS

Norma Johnston

AVON BOOKS ◆ NEW YORK

For Hella Reeves
and in memory of
Louisa May Alcott

AVON BOOKS
A division of
The Hearst Corporation
1350 Avenue of the Americas
New York, New York 10019

Copyright © 1997 by Dryden Harris St. John, Inc.
Interior design by Kellan Peck
Visit our website at **http://AvonBooks.com**
ISBN: 0-380-97367-7

Library of Congress Cataloging in Publication Data:

Johnston, Norma
    Lotta's progress / by Norma Johnston.
        p.   cm.
    Summary: In 1848 when Lotta's family immigrates to Boston from Germany, they face all sorts of difficulties until they are befriended by the Alcott family, who have set themselves up as "missionaries to the poor."
    1. Alcott, Louisa May, 1832–1888—Family—Juvenile fiction. [1. Alcott, Louisa May, 1832–1888—Family—Fiction. 2. German Americans—Fiction. 3. Immigrants—Fiction. 4. Boston (Mass.)—Fiction.] I. Title.
PZ7.S774217Lo   1997   96-36023
[Fic]—dc20   CIP

First Avon Books Printing: June 1997

AVON TRADEMARK REG. U.S. PAT. OFF. AND IN OTHER COUNTRIES, MARCA REGISTRADA, HECHO EN U.S.A.

Printed in the U.S.A.

FIRST EDITION

OPM   10 9 8 7 6 5 4 3 2 1

Chapter One

The bitter wind that sprang up an hour ago was building toward a gale. It turned the rain, falling steadily since noon, into sharp, stabbing needles. The State House dome gleamed dully against a leaden sky, and the unpaved paths that criss-crossed Boston Common were seas of mud. Lotta Muller plodded through it grimly, her head ducked into the upturned collar of her knitted jacket. The rain ran down her neck and between her hunched shoulder blades. Her skirt was splashed with the dun-colored Massachusetts mud.

What difference did it make now? What difference had *it made?* A cold rage was building inside Lotta's chilled body. Mutti had made the dress for Lotta out of one of her own, cutting the pieces carefully to avoid spots that were faded or worn. The skirt was skimpy because Mutti had had to squeeze frocks for Tilda and Lena out of the fabric, too.

"Thank the *Gutt Gott* that Tilda's small for her age, and Lena's only four. I can stretch the fabric for them with pieces from my blue plaid apron," Mutti had said to Lotta as she'd ripped the seams of her dark brown cambric the week before they'd sailed. "Karl will have Vater's smocked shirt made over for him,

1

and Pastor's wife has given me a bit of tan cambric for a shirt for Hansi. But you, Daughter—!" Mutti's eyes had rested fondly on Lotta. "You have shot up like a field flower since your twelfth birthday last April! It's a good thing the ocean crossing will take only six weeks, or your hem would be up above your knees before we land in Boston!"

Lotta loved it when Mutti called her "Daughter." It meant not only *a* daughter, but *eldest* daughter, and more and more lately, Mutti had been treating her that way, as someone old enough to understand things kept from the other children. Karl was fourteen, and the eldest son, but sometimes Lotta felt as though their ages were reversed. Karl had inherited all of Vater's impatience and stubbornness. And Vater certainly didn't confide in Karl! They could scarcely look at each other without anger.

All the same, Vater had told Mutti she could cut down the smocked shirt, the first thing Mutti had made for him after they were married, for Karl. And Mutti had cut up her own wedding nightgown to make a fine broadcloth shirt for Vater. "We must all look our best when we step ashore in our new country and are met by Vater's friend Herr Weiss," she had said to Lotta as she'd sewn with exquisite small stitches.

Lotta had put down her own basting impulsively. "*You* should have a new dress, too, Mutti!"

Mutti had shaken her head. "It is not possible. Besides, it is Vater who is important, he is head of the family and going to a new position. And you and Karl, because you will be entering a real school." She had smiled. "That is why, Daughter, you are to wear this—when you go ashore and when you enter school!" And she had put into Lotta's hands her most prized possession, the sheer lawn drawn-work apron Grossmutter Lindmeier had worn at her wedding, and Mutti at hers, one of the few things Mutti had been able to rescue when everything else had been lost.

"Mutti, I can't wear that!" Lotta had gasped.

"Ja, you can. And you will take care of it, for *your* wedding, and *your* eldest daughter. A keepsake of your new life in this New Jerusalem we have heard so much of, this land of promise!"

It had sounded so grand when Vater had talked to them about that dream, that promise, Lotta thought, pulling her collar higher and lowering her head against the beating rain. But the dream had burst like bubbles in the wind.

Lotta couldn't even remember exactly when Vater and his friends had started talking about Boston, city of the Puritans who also had braved the wild Atlantic in search of freedom. Boston . . . America . . . where the streets, folks said, were paved with gold. Where schools were public because *everyone* was expected to read and write, to take advantage of America's opportunities.

Some opportunities! Lotta thought savagely.

Maybe there had been opportunities in Boston in 1630, when the Puritans had landed. But this was November 1848, and after two months in Boston, Lotta knew that the streets were paved with cobbles if they were paved at all. The only gold she had seen was on the State House dome. Opportunities were only for the native born. The bad fortune that had dogged the Mullers through that last terrible year in Germany had followed them even here. Vater's friends, Vater's promised job, all had vanished. And as for school—

How am I going to tell Mutti? Lotta wondered. *That* was what had kept her stumbling blindly around the city ever since morning, kept her from going home after Karl had run off. For if America meant freedom, safety, and a job to Vater, to Mutti it meant one thing: *education.* In America it wouldn't matter that the Mullers were not gentry. Her children would be able to go to school.

In Germany, Mutti had taught the three older children their reading, writing, and ciphering. At least, she had taught Lotta and Tilda and tried to teach Karl. But Karl didn't see the need for book learning and didn't want to be taught by *any* woman, let alone his mother. Mutti could read and write because her father, a pastor, an educated man, had taught her. Mutti had walked methodically up and down Boston's twisting streets until, yesterday, she'd found a building that had had the magic words "Public School" chiseled in stone above the doorway. Lotta, who had picked up some English during the ocean crossing, had written out the words for her to watch for. Mutti had been pleased to see a gentleman leading a group of boys Karl's age inside.

Last night Mutti had argued with Vater till she'd convinced him Karl could earn more money for the family if he had some education first. Vater had ordered Karl, in very blunt language, to try. Because the weather had turned cold, Mutti had sat up all night knitting a jacket for Lotta from wool carefully unraveled from Vater's second-best sweater. This morning she had supervised their scrubbing under the pump out back and had plaited Lotta's pale blond hair lovingly.

"This is a morning you must always remember," she had told Karl and Lotta solemnly, sending them off with a kiss.

Remember! Lotta shuddered. Her stomach churned from shame and anger as much as from hunger pains.

The handsome stone building had been so quiet when she and Karl had arrived. Karl had squared his shoulders, pushed the door open, and marched in, with Lotta trailing after. They were in a deserted space, all dark, polished wood. Marble busts stood on pillars in the corners. A low, measured sound of voices came from behind closed doors. Karl had marched to the nearest one and thrown it open.

Fourteen pairs of young male eyes turned to stare at them. So did the teacher, tall, stern, and gray-bearded. The look in his eyes had made Lotta shrivel inside. But Karl had marched straight up to the teacher, clicked his heels, and bowed.

"*Guten Tag.* Here are Karl Muller and his sister Carlotta, come to enroll." He said it in German, of course. The teacher

4

frowned, and someone snickered. "My sister will explain." He had bowed again, indicated Lotta, and stepped smartly to one side.

In the best English she could manage, Lotta translated. The words came out in her thick accent. *"Herr Professor,* Ve—*mein Bruder* and I—ve come to go to school—"

She had faltered before the distaste on the teacher's face. She looked away and read scorn, disbelief, and amusement in the class's eyes. Lotta could understand a good deal more English than she could speak, and she heard too clearly the casual, cruel whispers: "Dirty foreigners . . ." "Can't even speak English . . ." "Don't belong here . . ." "Look at their clothes . . ." Over the whispers, the teacher's precise, colorless voice droned on.

How could she tell Mutti what he'd said? Schools in Boston were public, but they weren't free. They were only for those who were prepared, as immigrants were not. They were for those who spoke English . . . and Greek . . . and Latin. *Not* German; classes weren't taught in German. And they weren't— at least this one certainly wasn't—for girls.

Karl couldn't understand the words, but he sensed their meaning. He had drawn himself up, clicked his heels, and snapped out a sentence that brought color to Lotta's face and she would not translate. *Everyone* had understood Karl's swift, cutting gesture. *He* was rejecting *them.* He had pivoted and marched out. Lotta had willed her chin not to tremble. Head high, all the scorn she could summon in her eyes, she had walked out after Karl.

When she reached the street, Karl was nowhere to be found.

She could not go home, not till she'd worked out what to say to Mutti. Not till she'd found Karl. Only she hadn't found him, not near the Common, nor on the twisting side streets, nor in the Market near the waterfront, where he liked to loiter in hopes of work. And the sun had risen high and then darkened, and the rain and then the wind had come.

The sky was very dark now. She *must* go home. Mutti would be worried.

She couldn't go home without Karl. She knew too well what could happen if he wasn't there when Vater came in. It wasn't good for Mutti to be upset, with another baby coming in a few more months.

She *must* go home before dark. Otherwise, she wouldn't find her way in the narrow, ill-lit lanes where Boston's huge new immigrant population was crowded into too few houses.

Suddenly she was terrified of having to find her way home in the dark.

Lotta took a deep breath, pulling her sodden sweater tighter around her and squeezing her eyes against the salt of tears and the bitter rain. She had, she discovered, been standing half bent over, against a tree. She straightened, ducked her head against the rain's onslaught, and started out again along the footpath that was nearly invisible under muddy water.

Something rock-hard hit her in the forehead. She lost her balance and went down into the sea of mud.

· Chapter Two

November 1848

Lotta pushed hair and mud out of her eyes as a figure loomed beside her.

"Holy Mary an' all the saints! Can't ye watch where yer goin', ye silly fool?"

The words were English, but the accent was as thick as hers, only different, and the voice was young and male.

Lotta struggled to rise, her eyes blazing. "Vy you not vatch vere you ist going, *Dumkopf?*" she snapped.

"Mither o' God, it's a gurrl!" Hands grabbed her. Lotta fought them off.

"Don't touch me!" She shouted it in German, but the meaning was clear. His hands released her quickly.

"Sure, an' 'tis only tryin' to be o' help, I am—" The voice broke off in astonishment. "'Tis *you*, is it? Watcher way off here for?"

She stared. Bright blue eyes stared back at her from a freckled face. "Doncher know me? An' us livin' practically in each ither's pockets, ye might say. Michael Callaghan, what has the honor o' livin' next door ter ye!"

It was the boy around Karl's age from the Irish family that

lived across the landing. Lotta nodded, knuckling the wetness from her eyes. "Lotta Muller. I am sorry."

"No need ter be. I run inter ye as much as ye inter me." Michael stared at her closely, and his voice faltered. "Are ye all right? Ye look fair done in."

"I look—for my *Bruder* Karl." Lotta said the words slowly, trying to make her English clear.

"Run off, has he? He's probably home by now, getting warm by those stinkin' stoves we all got," Michael said cheerfully. "Come along wi' me, now, an' I'll see ye home. Then our fathers can help look, if needed—"

"No! I haf to find—before *mein Vater* knows—"

Michael nodded as if he understood. "How about I have a look around? I'll have him afore ye gets there yerself, I betcha!"

Relief flooded over Lotta. "Vould you?"

"So long as yer doesn't tell me mither I was invokin' the Holy Mither an' all the saints. You go along an' soothe yer mither's nerves." Michael looked her over critically. "Better brush yerself off first, an' take that tree outer yer skirts, or ye'll scare her witless."

Lotta looked down. A broken branch that had blocked her fall was caught in a three-cornered tear in Grossmutter Lindmeier's apron. She freed herself without speaking, her eyes welling. Michael gave her a pat on the shoulder.

"Git along wi' yer. I can find yer Karl, I'm sure o' it." He stood watching till she was safely off the Common and on the fine paved road that bordered it.

Darkness had fallen by the time Lotta found the lane where the Mullers lived. It had no name, so far as she knew, and it wasn't paved. During the rain the whole lane was an open sewer. Lotta picked her way carefully, glad she couldn't see what she was stepping in. Unlike the fine homes near the Common, the two rows of houses fronting on the lane were part wood, part brick. They looked as if they'd been thrown together hastily to house the wave of immigrants that was crowding the old Puritan city. They were all connected, and the walls between houses, as well as between rooms, were thin. You could hear and smell almost everything that went on elsewhere in the building. The Mullers' only privacy was the fact that among the eight families living in the fourth building on the left, they were the only ones who spoke in German.

The smell of smoke, coal, and cabbage met Lotta as she entered. For a moment, as sharp and clear as though she could really smell it, she remembered the hay and wild thyme scents of the meadow back home. *Back in Germany*, she corrected herself swiftly. The meadow, like the house, was gone. Although the meadow grass might have grown back by now—

She fairly ran up the two flights of stairs to the Mullers' door.

It's not a home, Lotta thought viciously. *It's a room. Our house was small, but it had four rooms, two up, two down, and poppies grew in the thatch of the roof. Why did Vater have to get himself in trouble? Why does Mutti have to be having another baby, when there are two grownups and five children living in the room already? When is Vater going to find work and move us to something better, as he keeps promising?*

How am I going to tell Mutti about the school?

She reached their landing and opened the door. The room's one lamp was lit, and by it Mutti sat sewing, as a pot of cabbage soup simmered on the stove. In Boston as in Germany, cabbage was cheap. Mutti looked up, anxiety turning to relief in her gray-blue eyes.

The words burst from Lotta before she could stop herself. "I ruined Grossmutter Lindmeier's apron, Mutti. And for nothing. The school won't take us."

Mutti rose. "It's all right, Lottchen. Sit by the stove and take those wet clothes off, and then tell me. And where is Karl?"

"He ran off. After. He was angry."

"And glad to get away from school," Mutti finished wryly. She warmed Lotta's flannel nightgown before the stove, then dropped it over Lotta's head so she could undress beneath it. Mutti hung Lotta's wet clothes on the line beside the window,

9

then sat down and patted the seat of Vater's chair. "Now, Daughter, sit and tell me, quietly."

Lotta did so, keeping her report to the reasons the teacher had given. "I'm so sorry about the apron, Mutti," she finished.

"Aprons can be mended. And you children can still study—here, if not in school. Next year there will be money for school charges."

"I don't see how—"

"*Next* year," Mutti said. She scooped some of the thin soup into a bowl and handed it to Lotta. "Sit. Eat. Your father and Karl can eat when they appear. See? I was lucky. We have a carrot today to go with the cabbage. And bread."

She held the loaf to her chest and sliced it toward her in the European fashion. Tilda, who was eight, passed the food around. Cups instead of bowls for the younger children. One slice of bread apiece. The two chairs were saved for Mutti and Vater; the children sat on the straw-filled mattresses stacked on top of each other against the far wall. Later, they would be spread out. One for Mutti and Vater. One for Karl and six-year-old Hansi. One for Lotta, Tilda, and Lena, who was four.

"The baby'd better be a boy." The words slipped out of Lotta unconsciously. Mutti looked amused.

"Yes, it would be convenient. But we shall love whatever comes. A good omen, a new child in a new world."

"Even the bread was better back home," Hansi said.

"You mustn't say that," Tilda said primly. Hansi stuck his tongue out at her.

"Why shouldn't I? It's true!"

"Children! Now that we are safe in America, we forget to be grateful? And strong? If we lived through the storm on the ocean, we can live through cabbage soup and American bread, *nicht wahr?*" To Lotta's shock, Mutti's voice cracked. "We are here—*together.* Have you forgotten the danger Vater was in, how brave he was? We should thank *Gott* every day that He has brought us through the troubled waters to the Promised Land!"

"Some promise."

Lotta thought she had only voiced the words in her head, but Mutti swung about. "You, too, Daughter? Have *you* lost faith, too?"

"I only meant the—the promise made to Vater didn't work out," Lotta said in a low voice.

"You must trust in God, Daughter. Or have you left your faith behind in the Old Country also?"

"Maybe we left God behind there, too."

Lotta hadn't meant for Mutti to hear that. She stopped, then realized with shock that Mutti *hadn't* heard. Mutti was bent over the back of her chair, coughing the rasping cough she'd developed since the weather had turned cold. Lotta ran to her. "Are you all right?" she demanded anxiously.

Mutti nodded, coughing.

Footsteps sounded outside on the stairs. Mutti straightened quickly, covering her mouth with her apron. "Don't tell Vater," she whispered hastily to Lotta. Whether Mutti meant about the cough or about the school, she wasn't sure. She crossed her fingers and hoped Karl had returned.

The door creaked. Footsteps went immediately to the pitcher of wash water. That meant it wasn't Karl. Vater didn't speak. That meant things weren't good. Mutti gave Lotta's waist a little squeeze and went to meet him. Lotta went to the stove and filled Vater's soup bowl. Tilda, who wasn't supposed to use the big breadknife, picked it and the loaf up and cut two slices. Hansi and Lena bent their heads over their cups and went on eating. In two months of living in one room they had all learned to give each other what privacy they could. Lotta set Vater's bowl and bread on the small table by Mutti's chair and curled up on a corner of the mattress pile, tucking her bare feet up beneath her nightgown. She could hear her parents speaking in low voices. Then Vater crossed the room and stood before her.

"Where is Karl, Carlotta?"

Vater was still drying his neck and arms with Mutti's monogrammed linen towel, and water glistened on his trim brown beard. His dark eyes, normally so kind, were grim, and his face was taut.

"Dieter, *Liebchen*—" Mutti began. Vater swung around.

"*Nien*, Mathilde. I want to hear Lotta's answer." He turned back to Lotta sternly. Lotta swallowed.

"Karl—did not come home with me." She improvised quickly. "He hoped someone at the Market might have work for him—Michael Callaghan knows places—"

"*Who?*"

"Michael Callaghan—the boy across the landing—" Lotta faltered as Vater frowned.

"I will not have Karl loitering with hooligans, getting into trouble—"

"Dieter—"

"*Nien*, Tilda! The boy knows he must not go anywhere without our permission. I will not allow—"

The door creaked again, ever so faintly. Vater's back was to the door, and he was deep in an argument with Mutti, so he didn't notice. But Lotta could see, beyond her parents' figures, the door open slightly. Karl was sliding in, his back flattened against the wall. Lotta dropped her eyes so they would not betray him.

"Here's Karl now," Tilda announced in a self-satisfied tone. Then she squealed as Lotta's pinch bit deep. "What was that for?" she demanded, injured.

"Mullers don't tell tales!" Lotta hissed fiercely.

It was too late. Vater swung round. His arm, strong from years of farm work, struck out with a cuff that knocked Karl halfway across the room.

Lotta jumped up so fast she knocked her soup bowl to the floor. She caught Karl just as he was rising, wiping a trickle of blood off his face and starting toward Vater with fury in his eyes.

"Mutti, Vater's soup needs rewarming. You see to Vater! I'll take Karl to the pump and clean him up." Lotta pushed Karl out the still-open door and slammed it shut behind them so fast she didn't have time to remember she was in her nightgown. She didn't care! All that mattered was that there be no more fighting. Karl was still dazed by the blow, so she was able to shove him to the stairs.

"Now, you listen, Karl Josef," she hissed through gritted teeth. "You go down to the pump and wash yourself off, you hear me? Look at you! Didn't being out in the rain all afternoon chill you down any? Have you any idea how you hurt Mutti?"

"I didn't mean to," Karl mumbled.

"You *never* mean to. Neither does Vater! But you do. Is this how you both mean to look after her?" Lotta gave him another push. "Now, go! I'm coming with you to make sure you don't run off again."

"Think you could stop me?"

"You want to find out?"

"I'm surprised you don't want to give me a bath like a baby," Karl said sheepishly, heading down the stairs.

"You act like one. Both of you. *Men!*" Lotta snorted.

They picked their way through the rubble in the lower hall to the back door. The rain was letting up, but there was no moon. Light from windows gave a faint glow that showed the pump. Lotta grasped the handle and pumped vigorously. "Now, *wash!*" she ordered.

As they reentered the house, a familiar figure was opening the front door, going out, closing it behind him.

"Vater, off to the saloon," Karl said with disgust.

"*Ja*, and for once we can be grateful."

"*He* hits *me* for upsetting Mutti?"

"Are you surprised?"

Karl sat down on the bottom step and stared at his knuckles. "I tell you, Lotta, if he does that once more—I am nearly fifteen years old, almost a man. Vater can't treat me like this. This is America."

"*Ja*, where the streets are paved with gold, and pigs can fly. If you want to be treated like a man, act like one. And not by fighting. By—" Lotta searched for words. "By being 'strong for the right,' as Mutti said about Vater when he stood up against the soldiers."

"And look where that got him. Got us." Karl stood up wearily and began plodding up the stairs.

It *was* easier when Vater wasn't there, Lotta admitted to herself with shame, when she was at last under the quilt between Lena and Tilda in the darkened room. If only Vater's friend, and the promised job, had been waiting for Vater when they arrived . . .

If only Vater didn't get so *angry* when he was worried.

If only Vater didn't go so often to the saloon. In Germany, Vater had sometimes had a stein of beer with his friends. But here—

If only she, Lotta, didn't feel angry so often. And worried.

She pulled the quilt up over her head so she couldn't hear the sound of Mutti's weeping.

Chapter Three

December 1848

"When will the *Kristkinder* come?" Lena asked, as she had been asking every morning for two weeks now. She asked it as soon as she awoke, which was whenever light began coming through the windows. Fortunately, the light came later and later. Winter had closed in on Boston, chill and cold. Another two weeks would bring the shortest day in the year. And *that* would bring the Christ Child's birthday, four days later. Lena had experienced four Christmases in Germany, and she liked what she remembered.

Only this year, Lotta thought as she shushed Lena, there would be no invitation to Schloss von Reisenthal, the Great House, to see the *Tannenbaum*, the tree lit with candles· and hung with chains of beads and little gifts. No doll for Lena, no nutcracker for Hansi, as there had been for Karl when he, too, was six. Baron von Reisenthal was gone from the Schloss to the cemetery beside the Lutheran church, and his nephew, who had inherited the Schloss, was not a giving man. Never again would Vater wake the children at midnight and take them to the barn to see if the animals really speak or kneel down to worship at the Christ Child's manger. The barn was

15

gone along with the Mullers' little house, and no one had had the heart yet to tell Lena there could be no Christmas for her here in the New World.

Lena asked her question again over their Sunday dinner of onions and potatoes. It was the one meal of the week at which Mutti still tried to live up to their old standards. She spread a quilt on the floor, lay one of her embroidered cloths on top of it, and set it with her own mother's silver. They knelt on the floor around it, even Vater, as though sitting together at a real table, and Vater asked the blessing as he used to do before every meal. He finished with the familiar words, "In the name of Christ we ask it." And Lena had asked, "When is the Christ Child coming?" and Vater had taken his napkin from his collar, folded it, and got up and walked out of the room.

Karl had looked at Mutti, his face sober. "Shall I go after him?"

"No, it would shame him. Let him walk until he has walked his way through his mood," Mutti said. "If you really want to help, take the young ones for a walk later. The air will do them good. You may meet Vater while you're out. If not, he will come home on his own. Tilda, will you please pass the bread?"

Karl and Lotta looked at each other. Karl's face mirrored what Lotta was thinking: *maybe he'll come home; maybe he won't.* Lotta shivered. More and more lately, Vater "wasn't himself." That was how Mutti put it, but Lotta knew it meant Vater had been drinking. Sometimes he came home rather vague and dazed. Sometimes he came home looking terribly sad. Sometimes he came home angry, and that was the worst of all.

Mutti rose to her knees. "Has everyone eaten? Karl, there are two potatoes left. You and Lotta each take one. We have no icebox here to keep them in, so they would spoil."

"Or a rat would get them," Hansi said cheerfully. "I like rats."

"*Hansi!*"

"Well, I do, Mutti," Hansi said, undiscouraged.

"You take the potato, Mutti," Lotta said hastily. "I'm not hungry." That was a lie, but Mutti needed it more. Lotta just hoped her stomach wouldn't start squealing.

Tilda began scraping the dishes into the slop pail. "Put the plates and silver in the washtub," Mutti directed. "I'll take care of them while you're out walking. Now we will read." She rose to her feet, clumsily—the baby was due in about three months—and took from the trunk the precious Bible that had been her father's.

First, Mutti read a chapter aloud. She was following the Advent calendar of readings. As soon as the Christ Child's coming was mentioned, Lena popped in with her question. This time Karl cut her off. "Listen, and maybe you'll find out," he told her.

After she finished reading, she passed the Bible around the circle and had them each read a verse aloud in turn and tell what it meant. This was the way Mutti taught them every day now; short chapter or long, round and round the Bible traveled until a chapter reading was completed. Mutti, Karl, and Lotta each helped one of the younger children. Lena snuggled her round body against Lotta, and Tilda sat by Mutti. Hansi was proud to have Karl helping him, but he didn't like it when Karl got impatient.

"Why can't Vater help me?" Hansi complained.

There was an awkward silence as it dawned on Karl, Tilda, and Hansi that Vater was never home when the readings took place.

"He has more important things to do than to teach reading to a stubborn boy." Karl frowned at Hansi in mock ferocity.

"You are very lucky to have an older brother who is as patient as he is with you," Mutti said.

"You *know* Vater doesn't like reading," Tilda said with a little sniff.

Lotta looked away. She knew the real reason, and not even Mutti knew she knew: *Vater couldn't read.* Little by little she'd

17

overheard things, noticed things . . . the way Vater always passed written or printed matters over to Mutti "so you will know what they say also, my dear"; the way Vater always managed to be absent from the children's lessons, or from anything at which he might be called upon to read. The way he scoffed at Mutti's insistence on the children's education, and sided with Karl about school, saying a man had more need of real work experience. But she hadn't added anything up until the day they'd come ashore on Boston's Long Wharf and Vater had led the family through the immigration line.

A stout man puffing a cigar had sat self-importantly behind a table with the ship's papers spread out in front of him. One by one, each head of household had to report to him. The line snaked endlessly. At last it was the Mullers' turn. Mutti stood behind the children, keeping them in order. Lotta, not Karl, stood with Vater because it was Lotta who had learned some English while on shipboard. The official spoke no German. As he rattled off his questions and then, with impatience, repeated them more slowly, Lotta translated them to Vater as best she could. It was she who had spelled out for the official their full names and places of birth and had written it all on a bit of paper for the man to copy. When the official had asked Vater for certain papers, and the baptismal certificates that showed their birth dates, Vater had taken an envelope from his pocket and handed it to her to sort the papers out. He had stared into space as Lotta had translated his answers to the official's questions.

At last the official had set down his cigar and pushed back his hat. "That's all, then, Muller. Read this paper over or have that kid of yours read it for you, see if all's right with it. Then sign on that line there. Or if you can't read or write, just make your mark."

"*If you can't read or write* . . ." Suddenly the pieces clicked into place in Lotta's head and almost knocked the stuffing out of her. She had lifted the paper and read it carefully, then turned her back on the man to speak to Vater. "I've read it and it's all right," she said in German. "After . . . after you check it, either write your name on the line at the bottom, or make your mark." She had stepped aside but out of the corner of her eye had seen Vater pick up the offered pen and carefully, as if unused to holding one, make a ragged X upon the paper.

She had never told anyone—not Karl, not Mutti.

It explained a lot, she thought. Including why, when he "wasn't himself" or was what Mutti called "blue," he sometimes made sarcastic remarks about Mutti's book-learning, or how she'd married beneath herself. Sometimes he said those things anyway, only half teasing. Mutti always treated the remarks as jokes that couldn't possibly be true. *She* looked up to *him* in many ways, Lotta knew. They all did. Vater knew so many things that could not be learned in books. He was so kind, so caring. Unlike many men, he thought daughters were as valuable as sons. No wonder Mutti had fallen in love with him! Especially, Lotta thought, since his past had been so romantically tragic. Vater's father had been killed in the Grand Duke's army when Vater was only eight.

According to the village story, Grosspapa Muller had been killed saving the life of his commanding officer, Baron von Reisenthal's only son. Later, Lieutenant von Reisenthal had also been killed. The baron had offered Grossmutter Muller work in the Schloss's dairy and one of the workers' cottages. Vater had begun tagging along at the chief cowman's heels. Soon everyone had realized young Dieter Muller had a real way with animals. He could calm the wildest horse, control the most rampaging bull, train every sort of dog. Soon he had had complete control of the Schloss's herds and horses. And when he was not much older than Karl was now, he had fallen in love with Pastor Lindmeier's daughter. Grossvater Lindmeier didn't approve; he wanted better things for his only child. But after he died, his only child Mathilde had gone to the Schloss to be companion to Baroness von Reisenthal and romance between Vater and Mutti had bloomed. And Vater had never found the time—or the patience—or swallowed his pride enough, Lotta suspected—to learn to read.

And *that*, Lotta was sure—and was certain Mutti was sure—explained a good deal of why Vater was unable to find work in Boston.

Mutti could teach him, Lotta thought, watching as Mutti gently corrected an error Karl was teaching Hansi, without embarrassing Karl as she did so. If she had, it hadn't worked, and Mutti could guess why. Vater was so proud!

She must have been staring at Mutti, because Mutti suddenly lifted her head and looked straight at her with a quizzical expression. Lotta reddened. She adored Mutti and envied her patience, but sometimes that patience drove her crazy. It always drove her crazy the way Mutti could read her like a book.

Suddenly, like turning the pages of a book back to a half-remembered picture, Lotta was seeing Mutti as she had been more than a year ago, before the trouble, before the dark wings of hair that framed her face had shown threads of gray. She had been standing on tiptoe, her hands on Vater's shoulders, laughing at him in rueful exasperation. "You are such a *Deutsher Dieter!* Proud and stubborn! And Karl and Lottchen are exactly like you!"

"*Ja,* they're my children, all right," Vater had laughed. "Be grateful I'm not from Prussia! Remember Karl trying to be like the Prussian officers visiting at the Schloss last summer?" And he had imitated Karl imitating the rigid soldiers. Then his face had sobered. "I wouldn't like to see our Karl a soldier. Although it may come, Mathilde. It may come. And it won't be easy for Lottchen, growing up proud and stubborn. They're not qualities that make life easy for a woman. I wish she had more of your patience and serenity."

"Oh, I'm proud and stubborn, too," Mutti had teased. "I married you!"

And Vater had laughed again, and pulled Mutti into his arms, and kissed her. Lotta had pulled her head back inside the curtains of the cupboard bed she had all to herself as eldest daughter and vowed she *would* try to be more like Mutti. She had snuggled down under the featherbed, feeling wrapped in a cocoon of security and love.

"Lotta! Lottchen!"

Lotta started. Mutti was looking at her, the Bible in her arms, as Karl was bundling Hansi into his jacket and wrapping a scarf around his neck. Tilda was doing the same to Lena. "I asked you if you're going to the Common with the others," Mutti repeated. "If so, go quickly. Already it's growing darker, and it looks like snow."

"What? Oh—no. I think I'll stay in where it's warm." *Warmer,* she corrected herself grimly. And not by much. The Mullers could not afford coal to keep the stove going steadily. Which was just as well, because the whole house, with windows shut against winter, reeked of smoke from stoves and kerosene lamps, coal dust, and cooking odors. Despite how constantly Mutti cleaned, everything was covered with a thin film of soot and grease.

Mutti stood by the window watching until Karl and the young ones were out in the street. Then she turned back to Lotta, smiling faintly. "I'm glad you stayed. It's nice to have time with you alone, Daughter." She moved to the trunk where she kept her few treasures and bent to open it, then stopped midway with a little gasp.

Lotta ran to her. "Mutti—"

"It's all right. The baby just kicked me. He's in a hurry to be born, this one." Mutti was sure, from the amount of kicking lately, that it was a boy. "Karl was just like this. Can you imagine—if we have *two* Karls—?"

"Mutti, lie down!" Lotta slipped the heavy Bible from her arms and knelt beside the trunk. She opened the clasps and lifted the lid enough to slide the Bible in, then shut and locked the trunk without looking further. What was the use? Seeing what was there—and what wasn't—only made her homesick. She straightened the embroidered cloth on top and looked around. Mutti was lying on the stacked mattresses, so that was good. Lotta put a coverlet over her, then filled the teakettle from the water pail and set it on the stove. She opened the stove door, threw in a handful of precious coals, and stoked them. Dishes didn't get clean unless the wash water was hot, and if it boiled she would make Mutti a cup of tea.

She moved around quietly, folding the tablecloth, hanging the coverlet it had been spread on over the line that divided the one big room into separate sleeping chambers. She washed the dishes and stood them carefully on the shelf Vater had put up for Mutti along the wall. Just like the shelf back home . . . suddenly the scene she had remembered flashed back before her eyes.

"I felt so safe then," she thought. "That's the last time I *did* feel safe. Right after that the trouble started." She wasn't going to let herself think about that. She knew what Mutti would say: *Count your blessings.* She straightened as a thundering horde tramped up the stairs and slammed the Callaghans' door across the landing. "It could be worse," she admitted to herself, half laughing. "There are only seven, almost eight, of us." The Callaghans had ten children. And they were so cheerful! She wondered how they managed. Of course, they had two rooms to the Mullers' one.

Lotta made a cup of tea and carried it over to the mattress. Mutti opened one eye. "I'm awake. Just catching my breath." She patted her waistline. "This one's going to be a handful, I can tell you."

"When will he—" Lotta stopped and blushed.

"Late February, I think. I have spoken to Mrs. Callaghan, and she will help me." Mutti pulled herself up and winced. "The way he's acting, he wants to be a Christmas baby, and that early would be very bad." She sipped her tea gratefully.

"Mutti . . . what about Christmas?"

Mutti shook her head. "I am sorry, Lottchen. It will not be possible for Vater and me to make the kind of Christmas you are used to. You must not mention it to Vater."

"I can't stop Lena."

Mutti sighed. "It's my fault, I'm afraid, for having the Advent reading. Tilda and Hansi, young as they are, know better than to worry Vater. I didn't expect a four-year-old to start counting the days!" Her face softened. "I have asked Vater to keep watching for a Lutheran church while he is out looking for work. We cannot be the *only* Germans in Boston! And there was one place, I do not know which, that told him to come back tomorrow because there might be work! If so, we may have a Christmas dinner. If not, we will still have the *real* Christmas all the same."

"Christmas isn't Christmas without presents—" The words slipped out of Lotta's mouth without intention. She shrank as Mutti turned on her, eyes blazing.

"Carlotta Hannah Muller, is this you talking? Christmas itself was and is a gift from God . . . who has brought us safely here through storms and danger! As He brought the Pilgrims and the Puritans. As he brought the ancient Hebrews to the Promised Land! And you say it is nothing if you are not getting *things?*"

"I didn't mean—"

"Perhaps it is time you considered what you *do* mean before you let the words fly out," Mutti said distinctly, and turned away.

Lotta's eyes stung. *I didn't mean getting* things, *though goodness knows we need some! I meant presents and everything else . . . the Christmas feeling. The candles on the tree at the Schloss. Vater waking us to see the animals kneel. Vater being himself. Feeling safe . . .*

She reached for her knitted jacket and pulled it on. "I'm— going after Karl and the children," she said thickly, and hurried out.

She couldn't see well. She groped for the stair railing and

instead felt a rough, unfamiliar sweater. "Don't you ivver look where yer goin'?" a laughing Irish voice demanded.

Lotta blinked hard. "Michael?"

"Himself. An' yer not yerself agin, I'm thinkin'." Michael looked her over. "Where yer headin'?"

"To find my brothers and sisters."

"Then if ye'll not scratch my eyes out for suggesting it, I'll walk with yer. Nasty slippery it is on the cobbles. I think I saw yer big brother on the Common."

"That is Karl." Lotta started down the stairs, and as if she'd given permission, Michael followed. "I do not really look for dem," she confessed. "I try to valk off my black German mood—and temper. You do not know how bad it can be."

"Don't flatter yourself. Have ye nivver heard o' black Irish tempers? That's what I am, an' proud o' it." Michael held the outer door open and tested the steps. "It's not slippery yet. Race ye to Washington Street!"

Washington Street was one of Boston's important streets, where the gentry rode in carriages and fine buildings stood. They reached it at the same time and drew up, panting.

"Ye run well, for a girl," Michael said approvingly.

Lotta's eyes sparked. "*Nein*. I—run—*well!*"

"All right! All right! I won't go to war wi' the whole German Army! I'll nivver make that mistake agin!" Michael grinned.

They walked along Charles Street to the Common, and across it, past the tree where Lotta had fallen and beyond, to where fine new houses looked down from the slopes of Beacon Hill. They stared up at the gleaming dome of the State House and even climbed the wide steps to its imposing doors.

"If it weren't Sunday we could buy pretzels an' sit on the steps to eat them," Michael said. "No one can buy anythin' in Boston on a Sunday!"

It was surprising, Lotta marveled, how easy it was to talk with Michael. His words sounded strange, not like the English she had heard on the boat, more musical than either that or

German. But she could puzzle out enough to get the sense of it. If she didn't say the right words, or said them wrong, it didn't seem to matter. She just filled the sentence out with German. Since Michael had quite an accent himself, she wasn't conscious of her own German accent or any bad English grammar.

"We could not shop in Germany on Sunday, either," she said. "Could you, in Ireland?"

"Folks can buy *anythin'* in Ireland," Michael bragged. "Any time . . . *if* they have the coppers. Me mum says after God made Ireland He threw away the pattern, 'cause it was too close to bein' a paradise on earth." He sat down on the steps, locked his arms around his knees, and stared out across the Common. Lotta did the same.

"Vy did you leave, den?" she asked, not looking at him.

"Holy—I mean, my goodness, don't ye know nothin'? We came 'cause o' the Troubles, o'course."

Lotta jumped at the word. "You mean you—"

"I mean the potato famine, o'course! Some blasted blight or disease got into the potato crops, which, seein's potatoes what the poor folks, who's ninety percent o' the population, lives on, was like the comin' o' the wrath o' God. Only what come was the wrath o' the English who owns the land. Not only wasn't there food for folks like us to eat, there wasn't work for us to do workin' the gentry's fields, an' no crops left for them to sell. Leastwise, that's what they said when they forced us off the land an' burned our cottage. Only fifteen by fifteen it was, an' so low me da couldn't stand upright in it, but 'twas our home!" Michael said heatedly.

Lotta didn't speak. After a moment Michael went on, more quietly, turning his cap round and round in his hands. "Me da says the reason there's famine is 'cause the landlords sold all the crops there was to the English markets, so there was nothin' left for us. All I knows is Mam's baby died 'cause she had no milk. No warnin' the soldiers gave us, an' me granny, she died in the smoke when she tried to save her rosary from the flames."

Lotta wet her lips. "Mutti—Mutti saved our family Bible. She brought it vit us."

"So did ye—?" Michael asked gruffly. When Lotta didn't answer, he cleared his throat. "Ye know what I think? I think we should look out for each other, sorta. Keep each other from losing our tempers or sinking down in th' black muck. Irish an' Germans aren't natural enemies like Irish an' English are, see?"

Lotta nodded. Michael thrust out a dirty fist and they shook hands solemnly. "Like I said, too bad Boston's so bloomin' pious we can't buy somethin' to celebrate our treaty," he chuckled.

"Couldn't anyway, not vit'out coppers."

Michael reached in his pocket and proudly displayed several small coins. "Plenty o' ways to get 'em around the Market if a boy don't mind runnin' errands an' gettin' dirty."

"Could Karl?"

"Sure, if he keeps a lid on his temper," Michael said grandly. "There's things a girl can do, too. Helpin' at food stalls, an' such." He looked at her. "An' I wouldn't squeal ter yer folks, either, if ye didn't want it."

There might be a possibility of Christmas after all!

Chapter Four

On Monday snow fell, and Vater came home late to supper, grimy and exhausted but sober. He laid a row of coins out on the small table.

Mutti's eyes lit. 'Dieter—!"

"Work at a butcher's, down behind the Market, cutting up meat. It rubs me wrong to be cutting up dead animals instead of caring for them, but it's money. And they gave me bones to bring home for soup."

He showed Mutti a paper-wrapped package, and Mutti jumped up and hugged him. She said the same thing Lotta had thought: "There may be Christmas."

"At least something on the table. If we had a table. They'll keep me through Christmas and New Year's, and if I please them, they say, it will be longer."

The next morning he rose long before dawn, and washed, and went off looking more himself than Lotta had seen him look since they'd reached Boston.

In Mutti's reading class, the Advent readings went on, leading them closer and closer to the Christmas Eve chapter about the infant in the manger. Mutti gave the older children writing assignments to do with Christmas and had Hansi and Lena practice drawing their letters. Vater brought brown paper home from the butcher shop for them to write on.

Karl and Lotta both chafed at the lessons, because they wanted to be at the Market, trying to earn coppers. Michael had been right—there were chores children could do, although they weren't "regular work" and the pay was poor. Lotta watched a shopwoman's baby while she plucked chickens and another time delivered feathers for her to a milliner's shop. The main problem was getting away from Mutti and the younger children, especially after snow began falling. It made the Common, and the Market, look like scenes from paintings at the Schloss, and Mutti worried about her children being out in it, most of all the younger ones. Especially when Karl and Lotta, like Vater, came home later than she expected.

Karl knew what Lotta was doing. She had to tell him, because he might have seen her in the Market, and she needed his help to keep the secret. Karl had given her a lecture on the dangers of a girl going out working, but that was before he saw her hoarded coppers. He usually walked her home. What Karl himself was working at she didn't know, and she knew better than to ask. Michael had introduced Karl to some of the Market men; she knew this from Michael, not from Karl.

It was hard for Karl and Lotta to keep their secrets from Mutti. There was only so much "exploring the city" and "getting exercise" she could believe in, especially when the weather turned bitter. One snowy afternoon she refused to let them go out at all.

"With Vater working at a butcher's, we won't have to worry about food for Christmas Eve," Karl said to Lotta, as they walked to the Market the next day. The Mullers always had the holiday feast on Christmas Eve, in the German custom.

Lotta's heart lifted. "Then we can buy gifts for Vater and Mutti, as well as toys for the young ones! A warm shawl for Mutti."

Karl nodded. "Heavy gloves for Vater. I saw some."

And if I have enough coppers, Lotta thought, *I'll buy wool and knit a jacket for the baby.* The small store of coppers she and Karl were hoarding was growing.

Five days before Christmas, Vater came home so very late that Lotta and Mutti were alarmed, especially when they heard his steps coming up the stairs slowly and unevenly. As soon as he opened the door to their room, Mutti ran to him.

He wasn't "not himself." But his arm was in a sling, wrapped in dirty cloths that were stained with blood.

"Karl, more water from the pump! *Quickly!*" Mutti shouted. Lotta emptied the water pail into the teakettle before Karl grabbed it and set the kettle on the stove. She threw coal into the stove's belly recklessly.

"It's not bad. The knife slipped," Vater muttered through gritted teeth, as Mutti unwrapped his arm.

"Not bad? It's cut to the bone! Lotta, tear a pillowcase up for bandaging. Karl, find a stick to make a tourniquet," Mutti ordered.

He should see a doctor, Lotta thought shakily. But she knew not all the coppers in the house would pay for that. Thank goodness Mutti was skilled at nursing! And that the medicine case she kept locked in the trunk was well stocked.

The next morning, blood was still seeping through the bandage. The wound, when Mutti unwrapped it to wash it, was festering. All the same, Vater insisted on going to work. He hated the job, but he was glad to have it. And so he went, each of those last days of Advent, as the cold that held Boston in its grip grew fiercer.

Tilda picked up Mutti's hoarse cough and difficulty breathing. Mutti dosed her with medicine from the trunk and kept an anxious eye on the younger children. Karl escaped class that day by sliding half out the door before Mutti caught him and then pleading for the chance to make a few coppers by helping ladies cross the slippery streets.

"You'd think ladies who could afford help would stay at home or be driven in weather like this," Mutti commented. "But not these Boston ladies. They walk everywhere, even when they needn't." She shook her head, baffled. "All right, go! But be careful." She would not let Lotta out at all. "I wonder if I should dose you all with a tonic to ward off fever," she murmured, staring at the contents of her medicine case.

"I'm just fine," Lotta said instantly. She couldn't have Mutti's tonics making her queasy when there was still time to earn!

"I'm not going to be sick for Christmas!" Hansi said, just as quickly. "Not from fever nor tonic. *Yecch!*"

"It's not Christmas for a while yet," Mutti soothed.

"In four more days," Tilda interrupted. "I saw a calendar in a shop window. That means the feast will be the night after the night after tomorrow night." She lapsed into a fit of coughing.

Over Tilda's bent head, Mutti's anxious eyes met Lotta's. "I don't know what to tell them," she said in a low voice to Lotta later. "I was hoping they wouldn't realize—they will be so disappointed."

"You'll be able to make a Christmas feast. Vater's working at a butcher's." That was all Lotta could trust herself to say, for fear she would give away the surprise.

"*Ja*, Vater finding work is the best gift of all, *nicht wahr*, Daughter?" Mutti leaned over and kissed Lotta on the cheek. Then a look of surprise crossed her face and she laughed. "Johannes is happy, too. He just kicked me!" "Johannes" was the name she and Vater had picked for the baby if it was a boy.

Vater came home late that night, and he brought stewing meat and bones for soup, but he looked very tired. He moved stiffly, as if his arm and shoulder ached, and he didn't want Mutti to rebandage them. She did anyway, exclaiming with worry, "Dieter, truly, you *must* see a doctor."

"*Nein*, I will be fine. Just give me some more of your elderberry tonic, love, to kill the pain."

The snow stopped the next day, but Boston was a world of

ice. It clacked in the branches of the trees as Lotta picked and slid her way across the Common. She had had difficulty persuading Mutti to let her out, and Mutti had done so only because Michael Callaghan had promised to see she did not come to grief. Karl, of course, was long gone.

"Sure, an' 'tis fine sleddin' there is on the Common, Miz Muller," Michael said, with all his Irish charm. He demonstrated the meaning of his English words with gestures. "I'm takin' me sister Molly an' young Pat, an' I'll be glad ter watch out fer yer bairns also."

Mutti, after communicating with Mrs. Callaghan about the baby in gestures, had concluded that the Callaghans were "decent people, even though shiftless and dirty," and that maybe they couldn't help that, having ten children. She let Lotta and Hansi go with Michael.

"I'll watch Hansi for two hours while ye look for chores, an' then ye do the same fer me," Michael said to Lotta, as Hansi was joyfully sliding down slope on a cardboard box from a trash bin. "Can yer trust him not ter tell yer mither?"

"Ja, if I buy him a pickle to suck," Lotta said, and did so. She looked for Vater in the Market but couldn't find him. With Christmas Eve two days off, the Market was thronged with shoppers. Vater came home that night late, very late, and almost immediately fell asleep. So did Lotta; doing errands out of doors in this cold weather made her quite astonishingly tired. She woke in the night to find Mutti dosing Tilda with cough syrup.

December 23 was just like the day before, except that Vater came home even later. He threw himself down on the mattress and fell into a deep sleep, and he hadn't brought the usual packet of meat home with him.

"He is driving himself too hard," Mutti said, as she and Karl pulled off his boots. Her face was anxious.

On the twenty-fourth, when Lotta woke, the room was filled with a cold, gray light. She sat up, blinking. Mutti still lay in

31

a deep sleep under the coverlets, and Karl and Vater were both gone. Hansi had found the heel of yesterday's bread loaf, and he and Lena were each chewing on half. "I tried to give Tilda some, but she didn't want it," he said.

Lotta turned to look at Tilda anxiously. The pillowcase and the part of the sheet Tilda lay on were damp, she realized with a little shock. "Mama," Tilda murmured, through dry lips.

"Hush. It's Lotta." She stroked Tilda's hair back, feeling the heat of her sister's skin. "We'll let Mutti sleep, all right?" Tilda nodded. Lotta opened the trunk, found the medicine case, and measured out the tonic Mutti gave for fever. She did not dare leave the house until Mutti awoke. Then she stayed home anyway, for Tilda's fever was worsening.

"Thank goodness," she thought, "I bought Mutti's shawl the last thing yesterday." She had learned that Market prices would be knocked down during the last shopping hours on Christmas Eve. But the soft blue shawl that matched Mutti's eyes might be gone by then, so she had spent nearly all of her remaining coppers to get it. The whirligig for Hansi, the doll for Lena, and the jump rope for Tilda were likewise tucked away. She had expected to earn enough today to buy a knife for Karl. Instead, she huddled under the coverlet for warmth and to conceal the baby jacket she was knitting.

Hansi and Lena were restless, and at last Mutti let them go outside and build a snowman with the two small Callaghans. Little by little, Mutti was losing some of her prejudice against the Irish, although she still wished Mrs. Callaghan scrubbed her floor, and her children, every day as she did. And she didn't make quite so many objections to Michael, to Lotta's relief. Michael was her only friend. He made her laugh; he let her explode. And her English—or Irish—vocabulary had increased a lot since she had met him.

By four in the afternoon the baby jacket was finished and the sky outside was darkening. Mutti looked out the window worriedly. "Vater promised he would come home early. And where's Karl? Somewhere with the Callaghans, I suppose. I don't like him being so much with boys older than he is."

"Mutti, Karl's almost fifteen!"

"Not for eight months," Mutti said firmly. "He thinks he's a man already."

"They'll be home," Tilda said hoarsely. Her fever had gone down, but she still had fits of coughing. "They have to. For the *Tannenbaum* and the Christmas feast."

There was a pause. Then Mutti sat down on the mattress beside Tilda and stroked her hair. *"Liebchen,"* she said gently, "we'll only have broth for dinner unless Vater brings food. And the *Tannenbaum* was only at the Schloss. We won't see one here."

"We will! Karl said we will. He *promised.*" Tilda fell into a fit of coughing as Mutti's troubled eyes looked at Lotta over her bent head.

The darkness deepened and the clock kept ticking. It had been Grossvater Lindmeier's and had come to America in the trunk, well wrapped in coverlets. Vater had taught Lotta to tell time on that clock, and she had always loved its bright pink and yellow roses, its elegant swirls of gold. Tonight she hated it as it ticked off the hours. At seven o'clock Karl came in, looking like a snowman and stamping his feet.

"I'm sorry I'm late. Have I missed the blessing—" Karl broke off, looking around at the cold stove, the tablecloth not laid. "Where's Vater? Isn't dinner ready?"

"I'm afraid there will be no dinner until your father comes home," Mutti said carefully. "He must have had to work late— Karl!" He was bolting out.

"I forgot something. Put coal in the fire, Mutti! I'll be back as soon as I can!"

"I'll catch him, Mutti. Don't worry!" Lotta grabbed her jacket and scarf and ran for the stairs, slamming the door behind her. She could hear the outer door banging behind Karl three flights below. *He'll be in the Market,* she thought grimly. *So will Vater. Vater's working late—*

She didn't dare let herself think about what she feared. She didn't dare let herself think, either, about being scared of going all the way to the Market alone. If only Michael were with her! But she hadn't dared lose time by knocking on the Callaghans' door. She'd been so sure she could catch up with Karl; she'd been able to stay abreast of Michael when they'd raced—

There were lights in windows all around the Common and people walking along paths trodden in the snow. A few sleighs passed her, driven by elegant young gentlemen. There were lights in the windows of King's Chapel, and people were shopping along all the streets to the Market. In the Market itself, people were haggling over geese and chickens, and prices on signs had been marked down. Lotta did not see Karl anywhere, not even at the butcher's, as she'd expected. Nor did she see Vater. She caught at a butcher's arm.

"Herr—*Nein, Mister* Dieter Muller. . . ." She was so nervous that the words came out in her thickest accent. *"Wo ist—?"*

The man, busy with a customer, shook her off. She tugged at him again, urgently, and this time he looked at her. "You one of Muller's young ones? We had to let him go days ago. He hurt his arm and couldn't work."

Let him go . . . Lotta puzzled that out, and her temper began building. They had taken away Vater's job—*days* ago. Where had he been during all those days? She couldn't let herself think about that. She whirled on the man, her words tumbling over themselves and her voice loud. "Vater hurt himself vorking for *you*. You can at least gif him meat for his Christmas feast!"

"Sure, kid. Here. We may not sell it now, anyway." The butcher took a chicken down off its hook, wrapped it in paper, and handed it to Lotta. She nodded curtly.

What else would Mutti need? She felt in her pocket and was relieved when her fingers closed around the coppers left from her Christmas shopping. Prices were dropping steadily as customers thinned, and she was able to buy carrots and turnips, potatoes, a few apples, and a fat loaf of bread before her coins ran out.

She still had not found Karl. Or Vater.

Snow whipped her steadily. The Market was closing up, and she felt as though her legs were going to close up under her, too. She stopped for a moment against the brick wall of a business building and set down her bundle till she caught her breath. Then she wiped the snow out of her eyes and reached down again.

The bundle was gone.

For a minute Lotta couldn't take it in, but she knew what had happened. The Market wasn't safe. Michael had told her that; Karl had told her that. Someone had stolen the Mullers' feast.

She could not, *would* not, go home without food. But her coppers were gone and the Market was closing.

The Market was closing—Lotta's head jerked up and grimly, doggedly, she began making the rounds of now-deserted stalls. Just as she thought, vendors had been too shiftless to carry off produce that didn't sell. She found potatoes, a fat turnip, a few parsnips, and a limp cabbage and wrapped them in her scarf. Then she set off for home, too furious and alarmed to be afraid.

Karl will be home already. He'll have found Vater, and they'll both be home . . . she kept repeating it to herself like a prayer. By the time she reached the house, she almost believed it. She fairly flew up the stairs.

As she ran up the second flight, she could see Mutti silhouetted in their doorway. One look at Mutti's face and she knew the truth.

"Mutti, I'm sorry. I couldn't find—"

"Hush." Mutti pulled her into their room quickly and spoke in a low voice. "Don't wake the young ones. Did you find Karl? Or Vater?"

Lotta shook her head, not able to bring herself to tell Mutti about the lost job. "I couldn't find either. But I brought—"

She froze.

Heavy footsteps were stumbling up the lower stairs, and a voice was mumbling. A too-familiar voice, with something all-too-recognizably wrong. Mutti picked up her skirts and, heavy as she was with the baby, began to run down the stairs.

"Dieter, where have you been? Lotta went to look for you, and we've been so worried—" Mutti's arm went around Vater's waist as he stumbled. "Lean on me."

Vater, the kind and tender, pushed her off so that she landed against the stair rail and almost fell. "I am all right! I do not need to lean on a woman!" He came up level with Lotta and leaned toward her, taking in her frightened face, her snow-wet clothing. "*You were out! Why?* You should have been looking after Mutti—"

"It's all right, Dieter. I sent her." Mutti fairly pushed Vater inside the room and shut the door behind them. "Sit down and warm yourself. Lotta, put coals on the fire and heat the broth for Vater—"

She straightened suddenly, and so did Lotta. Even Vater, halfway into his chair, jerked to his feet. Like a dream repeating, another set of footsteps were pounding up the stairs. The door flew open and Karl stood there, a large evergreen branch in one hand and in the other a parcel from which a chicken's neck was hanging.

Vater lunged at him; he was caught by Lotta and leaned forward, staring at Karl as though he were a stranger. "Where have you been?" he demanded.

Karl exchanged glances with Lotta and kept his voice level. "I went out to buy food for Christmas." He turned and handed the parcel to Mutti, who opened it and exclaimed, "Karl, how? It's a *beautiful* chicken."

Vater peered at it. "Why did you get one so small?" he demanded.

Karl stiffened. "At least I brought one! I *earned* it! What did you get with your pay packet, Vater? A bucket of beer?"

Vater, his face black with fury, lurched toward Karl. Lotta grabbed at him as Karl darted away.

"He didn't have a pay packet! He lost the job—" The words burst from Lotta before she could hold them back. Shocked into silence, she saw Mutti's stunned face. She heard Karl fling the bitter words at Vater.

"How did you lose it? Fighting? Or coming in drunk?"

Everything then happened very fast, though it seemed at the time as if it all went slowly, as in a dream. Vater lurched forward so swiftly that it sent Lotta spinning and pinned Karl against the wall. Somebody screamed. Vater's right arm let go of Karl to swing back into a fist. Mutti darted forward to protect Karl and was caught by the force of Vater's blow. She cried out. And Karl, stepping past her, coolly and deliberately punched Vater in the jaw.

Lotta screamed.

And then, suddenly, an Irish army burst in. Only it wasn't an army, it was Mr. Callaghan and his four oldest sons. They were strong and burly laborers, and they muscled Vater down the stairs and out of doors.

Lotta just stood there.

Hansi and Lena had awakened and were crying. Tilda was sitting bolt upright, coughing, her eyes wells of terror. Mrs. Callaghan had got Mutti into her chair and was putting a cold, wet compress on her bruised cheekbone. Michael came and looked at Lotta, and tried to get her, too, to sit. She shook her head mutely and just stood there.

She didn't dare speak because if she did she might scream to the housetops. Never, not even during the trouble, had she been so angry. Or so afraid.

From a distance, she saw Mutti and Mrs. Callaghan exchange glances.

"Frau Callaghan," Mutti said haltingly, "if you would be so kind—" She darted a glance toward Lotta. She had spoken in German, but Mrs. Callaghan understood.

"Sure, an' I'll look after yer young colleen for ye. 'Tis rest an' quiet ye need, Miz Muller, and the bairns will sleep, once they see yer all right. Callaghan will look after yer man fer ye. He knows just what's needed, seein's he's been on the sauce himself at times. Yer two oldest will come with me an' my bairns, an' I'll see they eat. I'll take them with us to midnight Mass, if so be's ye'll let them, seein' as yer black Protestants, I'm thinkin'?"

Mutti hesitated, then nodded weakly.

To Lotta's astonishment, Karl drew himself up tall, as he had at the school, and without any sarcasm at all, bowed. "Thank you for the invitation, Mrs. Callaghan. My sister and I will join you as soon as we have washed and dressed."

The Callaghans left. Together, Karl and Lotta separated the mattresses, spread the sheets, and hung the coverlets on the dividing lines. Lotta got Mutti to bed while Karl rewrapped the chicken, tied it firmly with twine, and hung it out the window to keep it cold. In the dark they washed, put on their best clothes, and went to meet the Callaghans, with Lotta wearing Mutti's red shawl. They all walked through the darkened streets to the Catholic church.

The church was lit with candles and full of people kneeling, full of music. It, and the service, were alien, strange, beautiful, and frightening all at once. Lotta, kneeling between Karl and Michael, loved the incense and the candles, hated the grim faces on the statues of suffering saints, shivered at the gaunt Christ on the altar cross. She shut her eyes tightly as though walling it all out. But the thoughts that she wanted to avoid kept crawling into her brain like worms. If there *was* a God, why was there all this suffering? Maybe it was better not to believe in God at all . . .

Chapter Five

January 1849

At midnight on December 31, the bells of Boston rang in the new year. Lotta knelt by the window listening, wrapped in Mutti's red shawl and shivering.

The year of the trouble was over. Now it was 1849, the year Vater had promised would be their good-luck charm, their new beginning. But it had all been a lie, or at best, a dream. Boston might be the New Jerusalem, a promised land—but not for the Mullers. They were "foreigners" here. A hateful little voice inside Lotta's head told her they always would be. Only Johannes, or Johanna, would be born here, a "real American." *But what,* she wondered bleakly, *about the rest of us. What about* me?

The room was icy cold. A faint sound of carousing carried up to her from the lane. It was Michael's big brothers and their father, maybe; she had seen Mr. Callaghan earlier and he was, as Mrs. Callaghan put it, "on the sauce." And Vater?

Lotta tried hard to blot out the hateful inner voice that raised the question, for she didn't want to think. She didn't think she could stand to worry anymore. All she wanted to do was go to sleep and dream of being safe and warm. But sleep wouldn't come.

On the mattress where her parents always slept, Mutti now slept alone. Vater had not come home on Christmas Day; he had not come home since. "He will come when he is himself again," Mutti had said privately to Karl and Lotta on Christmas morning. "Right now he is full of shame because he could not provide."

"Full of the sauce, you mean," Karl had blurted, and then quailed before Mutti's eyes. Mutti had cooked Karl's chicken and Lotta's vegetables. Karl had set up the evergreen bough as a *Tannenbaum*, and he and Lotta had hung it with bits of this and that. They had put out the children's toys, and Mutti's soft blue shawl, and had had on Christmas Day a celebration. But Vater's new gloves remained wrapped in paper. After two days, Mutti had put them in the trunk so they didn't see them constantly as a reminder.

As if we need things to remind us of Vater! Lotta thought scathingly.

After three days, she had begun sleeping on the mattress with Mutti. She told Mutti it was because both Tilda and Lena now had bad colds, but actually, she was worried about her mother. What if the baby started coming and Vater wasn't there? In Germany, when each of the younger children was born, Vater had fetched the village midwife and the other children had gone to stay with Pastor's wife. But everything was different here.

After Christmas Day, Mutti had even given up on the daily lessons. Lotta stopped going out looking for chores because she was afraid to leave Mutti. Karl went to the Market every day and brought back food. But he came home later and later, and he acted strange.

He became angry when Lotta peppered him with questions. "You look after Mutti and the young ones, and let me alone. I'm bringing food home, aren't I? It takes a lot of time to do that!"

"You should be looking for Vater!"

"Why? If the Callaghans, who know ever saloon in the city, can't find him, how would I?" Karl demanded. "And stop looking like you want to scratch my eyes out. Mutti's right. When and if Vater's ready to come home, he'll come."

"*What do you mean, 'and if'?*"

Karl just looked at her. "Vater's friend Herman Weiss just disappeared, didn't he? How do we know—"

Lotta flew at him.

What was scary, Lotta admitted to the stars that twinkled as cold and bright as chips of ice, was that Karl hadn't fought back. He'd just caught her hands, and brought them down, and held them. "You look after Mutti and the young ones," he said quietly. "Don't worry. I'll see we get enough food. I'm the man of the family now."

What else was scary was that Mutti hadn't challenged him about his absences. She didn't cry; that didn't surprise Lotta, because Mutti was always strong. But she let Karl's being out later and later, and his being secretive, pass without questions, and that was new and frightening.

As the bell music heralding the birth of the new year died away, Lotta crept back beneath the coverlet and snuggled into the hollow of Mutti's back. She wished she could pray, but the place inside herself where God had been was empty.

During the first week of the new year, winter closed in on Boston, harsh and cold. Winds whipped bits of ice across the Common, and the lane on which the Mullers lived was choked with snow. Going out back to the outhouse was impossible; emptying the slop buckets daily was a ghastly chore that Lotta was profoundly grateful Karl undertook. The back lot became like a frozen sewer, with stray dogs and rats scavenging. The lane itself, and the building fronts, veiled with white, took on an austere beauty.

By January 4, Lotta was afraid she would scream from the pressure and the silence. Mutti didn't mention Vater. The younger children didn't mention Vater or question Karl's being out so much. "It's not healthy," Lotta thought, remembering how Mutti had once told her that bottling up dark moods, or exploding with them, could be equally bad. "Like when I was bottling plums, and the pressure in the jars was too great, and they exploded, remember?" Mutti had said. "It can happen to people, too."

Maybe that's what happened to Vater, Lotta thought. And it was all too apt to happen to the rest of them—in more ways than one. With eight families all cooped up in the house—two to each floor, one in the basement, and one in the attic—and all windows shut, the fumes from cookstoves and lamps were as bad as fumes from sewage in the street had been. She began opening the window a crack to let in some fresh, cold air. And she herself took out the Bible and began giving reading lessons—and what English lessons she could—to the younger ones. Tilda's fever was over, but she and the others mostly stayed in bed, huddled under the coverlets to keep warm. The coal supply was almost gone.

On the Sunday after New Year's, as the lesson was in progress with Mutti listening quietly from her mattress, heavy footsteps clattered up the stairs. Karl? Vater? Lotta's eyes met Mutti's swiftly.

"You go," Mutti said hoarsely, and began coughing. Lotta flew to the door. But when she opened it, no one stood there, only two buckets heaped high with coal.

"The Callaghans," Mutti said weakly, when Lotta told her. "Bless them, they really are good souls." She coughed again.

Lotta stared at her, then felt her forehead. "You're feverish. I'll get the cough syrup and the tonic."

Mutti shook her head. "Could—hurt the baby. Get some snow from the windowsill . . . put it in a handkerchief on my forehead. My head aches."

Lotta obeyed, troubled. She made soup from the neck and wings of the chicken Karl had brought home the night before and made Mutti drink some. Chicken soup was a tonic that couldn't hurt anyone.

Inexorably, the clock ticked off the hours of the day. By the time Karl came in at eight o'clock, bringing bread, vegetables, and a chunk of beef, Mutti's fever was worse. Both Karl and Lotta were awakened in the night by Mutti's coughing. In the morning, as Karl was leaving, Lotta wrapped the red shawl around her and followed him out onto the landing.

"You must find Vater."

Karl gave a short laugh. "What am I, a miracle worker? Have Mrs. Callaghan take you to her church to pray to the saints, if you believe those superstitions!"

Lotta's hand came up and struck him sharply across the face. "Don't you ever say a thing like that again, you hear me?" she said in a savage whisper. Karl nodded, staring at her and rubbing his jaw. "If you're the man of the house now, I guess I'm the woman of it," Lotta swept on. "And I say if Mutti's getting sick, we may *all* get sick, and what happens to the young ones then? *Nothing* will get better until Vater's back. So just you don't come home tonight until you've found out what's happened to him!"

Karl just looked at her, his temple working. Then he turned and clattered down the stairs. Lotta went back into the room. Hansi was sitting up, staring at Lotta. The silence was broken only by the sound of Mutti's coughing.

By midday the younger children were coughing, too. I daren't get sick, Lotta thought, and tied a kerchief across her nose and mouth as she'd seen Mutti do when the children were ill. By late afternoon, Mutti's fever was worse and Tilda's had returned. Neither could eat any of the stew Lotta had made from Karl's good beef. After she and the young ones ate, Lotta fixed a plate for Karl and kept it, covered, on the stove. The stew pot, its lid tied on tightly, was hung out the window.

Karl did not come home.

The clock ticked by the hours until midnight and the fire in the stove went out, and still he did not come. Lotta, sitting up wrapped in the red shawl, dozed and woke, dozed and woke again. She went from being furious to being so frightened she was afraid to think, and then to being so tired she couldn't stay awake.

Her heavy eyelids closed and she felt as though she were falling down and down into one of the featherbeds on her wall bed back in Germany. And then, as clearly as though she could reach out and touch them, she saw them all together, around the fire in the cottage before the trouble. Vater looked so handsome, and Mutti so young. And Vater was smiling—

In her dream, a log broke on the hearth, sending forth a shower of sparks.

Lotta sat bolt upright, rubbing sleep out of her eyes.

She was in Boston, and the hands of the clock stood at seven-thirty. A wan light was coming in the window. She struggled to her feet and looked around. Karl wasn't there. Mutti was tossing in near delirium. She called Vater's name through cracked lips when Lotta spoke to her. Tilda had kicked off her half of the coverlet, and her forehead was burning up. Lena, too, felt feverish.

Lotta tied the kerchief over her nose and mouth and stared about her. Delirium fever called for cold baths. Whose need was worse, Mutti's or Tilda's? How could you tell? She moved onto Hansi's mattress. He sat up, blinking, at her touch, and he was not hot.

"Is Karl home yet?" he asked sleepily.

"No. I need you to go down to the front stoop and bring back a bucket of snow. Right away!"

"What for?"

Before she could stop herself, Lotta grabbed him by the shoulders and shook him. "Just *do it!*" She stopped, then knelt before him, shocked. "Hansi, I'm sorry. I didn't mean that. But you have to do it. I need you to, for Mutti."

Hansi, hiccuping, dressed himself and went.

When he returned, Lotta gave him food and forced herself to eat some. She almost choked on it, and her insides were churning. Then, remembering what Mutti had done for her when she had fever, she began laying snow on foreheads. She packed it against Mutti's body. If Karl was there she could send him to find a doctor somehow, somewhere—

Where is Karl?

Lotta didn't know she'd spoken the words aloud, but Hansi's voice, flat and accusing, answered her.

"You told him not to come home till he found Vater."

Lotta stared at him, and suddenly she was shaking all over. "Stay by Mutti," she whispered thickly, and bolted for the door. *The children mustn't see me break.* That was all she could think, all she could hold onto. Somehow, she managed to get the door open, slide out, and close it behind her noiselessly. Then she couldn't hold herself together anymore. She shook and shook, her hands pressed tightly across her face so she couldn't cry out, her forehead pressed against the wall of the landing so she couldn't fall.

When someone touched her, she whirled around, hoping against hope. Then her heart sank. It wasn't Karl; it was Michael, staring at her in astonishment and alarm.

"Fer the love o' all the saints, what's happened?"

Lotta swallowed hard to force back the lump in her throat. "Karl did not come home all night."

"So that's it, is it?" Michael smiled. "Sure, I've tried that a few times meself, an' me sisters never wept fer me. He'll be back, bright an' beamin'."

"You don't understand! Vater—Vater has not been home since Christmas Eve—"

Her words were coming out in a mixture of German and broken English, but Michael seemed to understand. He steered her to the top step and sat her on it, then sat beside her.

"Karl went lookin' fer him, is that the way o' it? He's a brave lad or a fool to have stayed out all a night like the last one. He'll be back—"

Lotta shook her head violently. *"You don't understand!"* she repeated. "I told him—not to come vit'out Vater—and now he's gone, too—and Mutti and Tilda burning vit fever—"

Michael stood up. "Me mither's out, but she'll be in ter help, soon's I can tell her what's wrong. Seamus an' I are home alone, 'cept fer the little girls, but if I stay wi' them, Seamus'll find out what's become o' Karl, ye can count on that. Now, will ye be all right if I leave ye?"

Lotta nodded. *None of you could find Vater when you went looking,* she thought, as she went back inside.

The clock ticked by the hours. A weak gray light filled the room, but at least there was no further snow. For once, Lotta was grateful for the room's damp chill. Everyone's fever seemed to be lessening. She doled out doses from the medicine chest. She changed the sheets on Mutti's mattress, got Mutti and Tilda into fresh nightdresses, and transferred Tilda onto the mattress next to Mutti. Then, with Hansi's help, she stood the other two mattresses up against open windows to air. She swept, then scrubbed the floor, shook all the coverlets out the window, and rehung them on the indoor lines so that Mutti's mattress was curtained off as the sickroom. It was hard work, but it made waiting for Karl go faster.

It was late afternoon when a knock came at the door. Michael stood there, alone, wearing his jacket and turning his cap round and round in his hands. Lotta stared at him and wet her lips. "You didn't find him."

"Aye, we did. That's ter say, Seamus found out where he is. Karl, not yer da. I thought ye'd rather hear the tale from me." Michael's eyes were kind. "Ye'd better step outside."

Lotta grabbed the red shawl from its peg and stepped out wordlessly, shutting the door behind her. "Tell me."

"Not ter put too fine a point on it, he's wi' the police. They won't let him go till yer da comes to claim him."

"*Vat?*"

Michael looked embarrassed. "Seamus couldn't press 'em, on account o' the police take too much interest in himself already, see? But he did find out the Law ain't seen hide ner hair o' yer father, dead or alive, if that's any comfort."

Comfort? Lotta's jaw set. "Take me dere!" she ordered.

Michael stared at her. "Where?"

"To de law, of course! Vater can't go for Karl, and Mutti's sick, so *I* vill!" She stormed down the stairs, with Michael behind her.

They scarcely spoke on the way. Michael hurried ahead, breaking a path through the snow, with Lotta running after. She pulled the red shawl up over her head and held it against her tightly. She was thinking hard. When Michael stopped at last before a looming building, she turned on him.

"Tell me de rest!"

"What?"

"*Vat* Seamus told you. I know dere's more from how you're acting." Her words came in breathless spurts and broken English, but she could tell Michael understood. He hesitated, then blurted it out.

"The police brought Karl in fer stealing."

"*Vat?*"

"A shopkeeper in the Market put th' charge against him," Michael said. "It's true, Lotta."

For a minute she couldn't breathe. She just stared. Then she flew at him, beating her fists against his chest. "*Liar!*"

Michael caught her wrists and jerked her arms down. "Hush! Ye want the police ter hear ye?"

Sure enough, people coming out of the building and a uniformed guard standing beside the door were staring. Lotta willed herself calm. "*They'll* hear me. Acting like a lady. You'd best go home, Michael Callaghan, since you think *mein Bruder* a thief. Or since the police are so familiar vit the Callaghans! I can find *mein* own vay!"

Head high, she marched into the building.

The lamps inside were lit against the afternoon dark. There was a bench with people sitting on it—men Vater wouldn't have liked, and a brightly dressed woman. She looked at Lotta with curiosity, then pity. Lotta jerked her eyes away and marched to the high counter.

What would Mutti say? How would she say it? Lotta held her head up and spoke formally. "Here is Carlotta Muller. I come for my brother Karl."

The words came out in a thick German accent, and the big uniformed man behind the counter frowned. Lotta repeated her words, speaking slowly and distinctly. The man looked at another, and they both shook their heads.

"Karl—*ist*—here. *Mein Bruder.*" She held up her hand to indicate how tall Karl was and pointed to show his hair was blond like hers, his eyes as blue.

The men spoke. Then the second man, tall and thin, bent toward her. He used English she could barely understand, but she recognized some words and shook her head. "Vater cannot come. He is not here." She crossed her arms and shook her head to indicate she did not know where he was. "Mutti—sick. I come for *Bruder.*" She could tell from their faces this was not good enough.

"I vant to see *mein Bruder,*" she demanded. When they began shaking their heads, she marched to the bench and sat down beside the woman in red. "I stay!"

The men spoke together again. Then the tall one came around the counter and beckoned to her. In silence, Lotta followed him down a narrow corridor and into a small room with a barred window. The man left. He came back, pushing Karl ahead of him, one hand firmly gripping Karl's upper arm. The man sat down on one of the room's two chairs, and brother and sister stared at each other.

Karl was filthy. There was a bruise on his face, and his wrists were chained together. But it was the look in his eyes that frightened Lotta most.

"How did you know I was here?" Karl demanded in German.

"Michael's brother Seamus. He found out."

"Seamus would know about jails," Karl said grimly. "I don't suppose he managed to find Vater, too?"

Lotta shook her head. "Only that he is not here. Not dead."

"That's something." Karl turned away. "You shouldn't have come here."

"When it's my fault? I shouldn't have told you not to come home till you found—"

"No! It's nobody's fault but Vater's! Him and his being 'not himself'!" Karl mimicked Mutti's tone savagely. "If Vater had been himself, I wouldn't have had to—" He checked himself abruptly.

"Had to what?"

Karl didn't answer, so she turned on him squarely. "What is all this? Michael said you're accused of stealing!"

"So he had to tattle, did he?" Karl said scornfully. He turned his back to stare out the window, and Lotta's temper exploded.

"Don't do that! Mutti's right, you try to be the big man— *look* at me!" She grabbed his arm.

The officer sprang to his feet and separated her from Karl forcibly.

"He's right," Karl said. "You shouldn't be here. Just go home."

"Without *you*? Without making this right? Haven't you *told* them that you didn't—?"

She shrank back at what she saw on Karl's face. Suddenly, even in this heated building, Lotta felt cold.

"How do you think you've been eating since Christmas?" Karl asked in level German. "*You* haven't been in the Market lately. There are no chores now. What else was I to do? Let you all starve?" He walked away and went on in a harsh whisper. "You always did want to run things, Miss Bossy. It's up to you now. They won't let me out of here till Vater comes to pay for the food and the fine. If he ever does come."

"*Don't say that!*" Lotta was starting to shake, as she had earlier on the landing. She willed herself calm. "You take care," she said carefully. "Don't get in trouble. I will look after everything." She turned and nodded abruptly to the officer, who rose to take Karl out.

"Don't tell Mutti," Karl said hoarsely.

Lotta nodded. She couldn't tell Mutti, not when she was so ill. She couldn't tell Karl about Mutti, either.

She took a deep breath and marched back to the front desk. "*Bitte,*" she said. "Please. Ve are good people. Vater *ist*—looks for work. Not here. Mutti sick. No food. No money. We need *mein Bruder.* Pay later."

The officer behind the desk shook his head.

The street outside was almost dark. Michael had gone, as she had told him to. "My miserable temper!" Lotta muttered to herself. She would have to find her own way home.

She had gone only a few steps when she heard a voice calling.

"Girl! Little girl!"

The woman in the bright dress, the one Lotta saw at the police station, came hurrying up and laid a hand on Lotta's arm. She looked older close up, and her face was painted like an actress's. But the black-rimmed eyes were kind. "I heard what you said in there." She opened her crocheted reticule and took out a few coins. "It's not much, but you need it more than I do, even. Take it."

Lotta battled with her pride. "Thank you. For *meine Mutter,*" she said stiffly. "Ve pay back. You gif me your name, please, *ja?* Vater vill thank you."

The woman pawed through her bag for a small pencil and a bit of paper. "Forget it. I'm Bella, that's all. You need more help than mine. There's a crazy lady come to town lately, goes around giving things away to poor folks. Food, and clothes. A gentleman friend of mine told me about her. He said she lives on Dedham Street. I'll put her name down for you." She scribbled hastily, then pressed the paper into Lotta's hand. "Maybe she can help you."

The woman nodded kindly, then hurried off into the darkness.

After she was gone, Lotta looked at the paper in the lamplight coming from a window.

Mrs. Bronson Alcott

Chapter Six

January 1849

Dedham Street looked the way the Mullers' lane must once have looked, except that it was a real street, wide enough for a wagon or a carriage. The houses were similar, narrow and four stories high, but of dark red stone. *Like that school we couldn't go to,* Lotta thought. A sudden fear clutched her. Would the "crazy lady" who gave away food look at her in the way Herr Professor had?

She couldn't let herself think about that; she had to keep going. It was already mid-afternoon and snowing hard. Lotta hadn't been able to start her search until she got Mutti to drink a little chicken broth at noon. In the morning she'd swept and scrubbed again, bathed Mutti and Tilda, both of whom were somewhat better, and aired the bedding. Then, leaving Hansi in charge of the invalids, she had started out.

One of the Callaghans told Lotta in what direction to head. Mrs. Callaghan had not been home—she was doing work in a factory somewhere—and neither was Michael. Just as well. Lotta didn't want an audience when she asked for charity.

After leaving the lane she'd turned left, as she'd been told to. From then on it was a matter of showing her slip of paper to everyone she passed. Some people just shook their heads. Others tried to explain. Lotta couldn't understand the words, but she understood the pointing fingers. It was over an hour before she reached the corner of Dedham Street and started down it. *Mutti would like it here,* she thought. The houses weren't grand, like those on Beacon Hill or behind the State House, with their fine carved doorways and old lavender glass window-panes. But the people who lived here, unlike those in the lane, were what Mutti would call "house-proud." Doorknobs were polished and windows gleamed.

The few people she passed looked blank when she showed the name on the paper. Perhaps the crazy lady who gave away food didn't really live here. Perhaps she was new. Perhaps she really *was* crazy, and the story about her giving things away wasn't true.

I won't think that, Lotta told herself sternly.

She began knocking on doors, showing her slip of paper to whomever answered. It wasn't till she reached the house on the corner of the third block that she had any luck. The woman who answered the door shook her head and rattled off something in English that Lotta didn't understand. She curtsied her thanks and was starting wearily down the steps when the woman reached out and pulled at her shoulder.

Lotta turned. The woman was smiling and pointing down into a little area below the steps where there was another door. Its knob and knocker gleamed brightly, and lamplight glowed behind muslin curtains in the low windows.

Lotta made her way down the steps, and down a few more into the areaway. She lifted the knocker and clanked it firmly, her heart hammering with it.

There was a sound of voices inside and then the door was thrown open.

A girl of about Tilda's age stood there, silhouetted against the inner glow. She had yellow hair like Tilda's, in curls drawn up with a sky blue bow. Her black sateen pinafore covered a dress of flowered calico, and her tiptilted nose was in the air.

"We aren't buying anything today. It's Sunday," she announced, in a voice much like Herr Professor had used.

Lotta's face burned.

"Abbie May!" and "Don't be so hoity-toity, Miss Priss!" exclaimed two feminine voices from inside.

The girl turned red. "I was only—" she started to say, and was given a swat on the rear by a tall young lady in a dark plaid dress with an ink smudge on her cheek.

"Yes, we know, May, but do stop trying to sound like Aunt You-Know-Who in her worst moments! It's bad enough when she snoots us!" The young lady turned back to Lotta, her dark eyes dancing. "I apologize for my sister. She likes to put on airs. May I help you?"

Lotta could understand only some of the words, but she understood the warmth. *"Frau All—kott?"* she asked. She produced her paper, and then she couldn't help herself. She started to shake. And all the time the words kept spilling out . . . about Karl, about Mutti and the baby and the fever, about Vater.

The tall young lady put up a hand. "Wait! I'm just Louy. You want my mother. Marmee!" she called into the house, pulling Lotta inside.

They were in a room that was everything Lotta had dreamed life in Boston could be. A fire blazed brightly on a clean-swept hearth. China plates that reminded Lotta of Mutti stood on the mantelpiece by tall brass candlesticks. A lamp was lit on a table covered with a cheerful damask cloth, and an open book lay facedown beside it. It looked like a home.

A sewing circle was in progress. From a rocker by the fire a stately dark-haired lady with coronet braids like Mutti's looked up brightly and asked, "Yes, Louy?" She had been sewing on a large white cloth that was spread across the skirt of her dark green dress. The girl called May knelt on the braided rug, stitching industriously on the other end of the cloth and trying not to meet Lotta's eyes. A gentle-eyed girl about Lotta's age stopped hemming to pat a three-legged stool beside her.

"Come sit by the fire! It's dreadful out. You must be cold." She smiled encouragingly as Lotta hesitantly approached. "How can I help you?"

"I think it's something about her mother being ill and having no food," Louy said.

Frau Alcott gave a shocked exclamation. "You sit down there by Lizzie, child, and warm yourself while you tell me slowly."

Lotta obeyed. Her shakiness was fading and she'd had a chance to organize her thoughts. She listed the Mullers' needs as slowly, clearly, and briefly as she could. But when she tried to explain about Karl being jailed for stealing food, she couldn't go on for the lump in her throat.

"That's enough. I understand." Frau Alcott rose in a rustle of petticoats and began taking things from a cupboard to fill the basket Louy handed her. "Fetch me the old blue blanket, May. Louy, a loaf of bread and some apples. And my notebook! Lizzie, get the medicine case. What street do you live on, child?"

"*Nein*, not street. Lane. No name. I vill show—"

"No," Frau Alcott insisted firmly. "I will find it. You will stay here with my girls and have bread and milk for supper with them. I hope I can return with good news for you. Louy, the map."

Louy opened a door into another room and Lotta, looking over her shoulder, gasped.

The far wall of the room was lined with rows and rows of books. Books like those at the Schloss, bound in black, brown, crimson, and green, and stamped elegantly with gold. Involuntarily Lotta followed Louy in, trailed by May.

"This is the drawing room," May announced importantly, sounding much like Tilda. Lotta paid no attention. She moved along the rows of books, drinking in the strange foreign titles. But not all so strange . . .

Lotta gasped again. There was a book of Goethe's . . . just like the book at the Schloss back home that old Baron von Reisenthal used to show her . . .

Reverently she drew the volume from the shelf.

Instantly May grabbed it. "Don't put your dirty hands on that, girl! It's my father's book!"

Lotta thrust her hands behind her back as though stung.

"*Abbie May!*" all three other Alcotts shouted.

May flounced. "The girl can't read it anyway. Besides, it's in German!"

Lotta drew herself up proudly. "I, Carlotta Elizbetta Muller, *am* German! *Und* I can read!" She flipped rapidly through the pages until she recognized a poem title, turned to the end, and closed the book. Then she recited her favorite lines, translating the remembered German into her best English as she did so.

To those people steady—*nein*, strong of mind—honor is due.

For *Gruss Gott* and the Laws, defending their families, their loved ones,

They faced down their enemies together, and fought to the death!

Louy took the English translation from the shelf, looked at it, and then at Lotta, and with the faintest trace of a smile read the book passage aloud.

For to those resolute peoples respect will be ever accorded,

Who for God and the laws, for parents, women, and children,

Fought and died, as together they stood with their front to the foeman!

"I guess Carlotta's just put all of us in our places," she said firmly. "I read and speak only one language, worst luck!"

"Well, I'll leave you in Louy's care, then, Carlotta, and you two can talk books together. In two languages! There's a German dictionary around here somewhere. And the map! I thought you were looking for that, Louy."

Louy hurriedly spread the city map out on the table. She, Frau Alcott, and Lotta all bent over it. Lotta pointed out the lane and Frau Alcott nodded.

"I know exactly where it is. And your brother is with the police near the Market? Then I'll be off. Lizzie, you and May spread that sheet out across your bed and sew on it in there. I hope to find it completely hemmed when I return."

"Yes, Marmee," the two girls chorused. Lizzie wrapped a shawl around her mother. May ran to fetch her mother's bonnet and gloves. Louy winked at Lotta.

"Trying to make up for her bad manners. She'll be an angel for the rest of the day now, probably," Louy said to Lotta, when they were alone. "I'm sorry about how she behaved with you."

Lotta grinned. "I haf sister. Mathilde . . . Tilda. She just like."

"How many of there are you?" Louy asked, filling a teakettle and setting it on the stove.

"Vater . . . Mutti . . ." Lotta ticked them off on her fingers. "Karl Josef, fourteen. I, twelve. Tilda, eight. Hansi, six. Magdalena—Lena, four. *Und* one coming. Johannes, Johanna—ve not know yet."

"Eight of you in one room?" Louy exclaimed, then caught herself. "Now *I* sound like May! When did you come from Germany? And why?"

"Is now six months ve left. Four months here. Dere vas trouble." Lotta stopped abruptly.

"Now *I'm* being rude! It's my abominable tongue! Marmee says I'm hopelessly nosy because I'm a writer, and that that's no excuse." Louy looked at Lotta's confused face and started to laugh. "Come on!" She caught Lotta's hand and pulled her into the drawing room. Together they found the German-English dictionary. Together they sat down on the floor before the fire in the back room and began looking up the necessary words.

"You are a writer?" Lotta was awed.

"I've been writing ever since I was little, Marmee says. Stories, poems. I'm writing a splendid story called 'The Rival Painters.' And plays. We put on my plays all the time when we lived in Concord. My sister Annie's a wonderful actress!"

"Annie?" Lotta asked.

Louy looked through the dictionary to explain that her older sister was now staying with Frau Alcott's relatives to teach their children.

"A teacher!" Lotta was again impressed. "Me, I teach de younger ones since Mutti is ill. But not *gut.*"

"You mean, not well."

"*Ja,* I teach vile Mutti not vell, but I not teach *gut.*"

Louy laughed. "English is awful sometimes!" she said, and explained that "well" had two meanings. "And I'll bet you *do* teach well. Where are you in school? . . . Lotta? Did I say something wrong? I'm sorry."

"Mutti vish us go to school, but ve not allowed," Lotta said carefully. "Not speak English. Foreign. And cannot pay."

"Well, if that's not the stupidest thing I've ever heard!" Louy exclaimed. "How does anyone expect you to *learn* English if you don't go to school? Although I do understand, sort of. Teachers need to be paid. Father was a teacher, and I know he needed it."

Lotta drew her breath in. "Your father vas a teacher?"

"He was, but not the one you had the misfortune to meet." They resorted to the dictionary again to explain that. "He was Herr Schoolmaster, too. But he always got in trouble, because people were too stupid to understand how wise he was."

"Like *mein Vater* at de Schloss." The words slipped out before Lotta could stop them.

"Like that, was it? Don't worry, you don't have to tell me." Louy smiled.

"Vat does your Vater do now?" Lotta asked.

Now it was Louy's turn to look embarrassed. "He writes. Things for himself, and for his friends. There are not too many people who understand him. He's a philosopher." They needed the dictionary again for that. Then Lotta nodded.

"Like Socrates. Like Plato."

"A lot like Plato. How do you know about Plato, Lotta?"

"Baron von Riesenthal, at the Schloss, before the trouble. He vas my—" She looked in the dictionary to find the word "godfather." Louy was impressed.

"I learned about Plato from Father, and from Mr. Emerson, who's been sort of a godfather to me, in a way. We don't have godparents in the Unitarian Church. Not that Father's really a Unitarian anymore, though Marmee is. Father sort of has his own church, alone in the woods with God. Are you Catholic, Lotta?"

Lotta shook her head. "Lutheran. Only no church here."

"There's one somewhere. Marmee will help you find it. That's what Marmee does," Louy said, her voice softening. "She helps people. And I write, and Annie teaches. She's going to open her own school next year, and I'm going to help her. Maybe you can come to it! And of course we all sew, even May, though she hates it. May and Lizzie go to school with a friend of Father's. Lizzie's musical, but we don't have a piano. I'm going to buy her one as soon as I'm rich."

Lotta, baffled, looked around her. "*Dis* is rich!"

"No, it's not. It's three rooms and kitchen in a basement. You should have seen the house we had in Concord! I had my own room, opening on a garden and the woods . . ." Louy's voice was wistful. Suddenly she jumped up, pulling Lotta with her. "Here we are talking away and it's 'most time for supper! I hope you like bread and milk. And apples! In any Alcott home there are always apples! Let's put some on the hearth and roast them."

She led the way back into the front room, which was also the kitchen, and began bustling about, a long black apron tied over her cheerful dress. The firelight danced on her thick chestnut-colored hair, turning it almost to copper. More copper gleamed on the pots and pans hanging by the stove.

"One good thing about this place is that we're on a corner. I can see everybody's boots and shoes trot by while I'm cooking and imagine what the rest of 'em looks like." Louisa laughed, indicating the high windows that were level with the sidewalk outside. "It's pretty funny in a rainstorm, I can tell you!"

"You cook, too?" Lotta asked, impressed, as Louy began moving deftly about, taking down a small blue-and-cream lidded pitcher and several plates, and turning the apples deftly.

"Who else? Marmee's out saving the Boston needy, Annie's away teaching, Father's just . . . out, talking philosophy with people, and the girls are in school. So I'm chief cook and bottle washer. It gives me time to write." Louy paused, a gleam in her eye. "Do you clean and cook, Lotta?"

Lotta grinned, too. "Who else? At least, ven Mutti's not vell."

Louy sat down and clasped her arms around her knees. "Fraulein Muller, I have a bargain to make with you. If you will come here and rattle pots and pans for me—I mean, help cook and clean—and teach me German, I will teach you English and other things. It will be practice for when Annie and I open a school next year."

Lotta hesitated only long enough to decide how, not what, to answer. Then she thrust out her hand as she had done with Michael.

Louy shook it firmly. "It's a bargain, then. Just between us women!"

A log cracked on the hearth, sending up a shower of stars.

Chapter Seven

February 1849

Frau Alcott got Karl released from jail. None of the Mullers was sure exactly how she had done it, but she had. Herr Professor had been involved in it, too, apparently. Karl was to report to him twice a day, morning and evening, at the room on West Street where Herr Professor held what Louy referred to as "conversations." These were, Lotta gathered, very lofty discussions of philosophy that Herr Professor led in which some of his intellectual friends participated while more just listened.

"Like university?" Lotta asked Louy, and Louy laughed ruefully.

"*Ja*, like university, only it doesn't pay as well." Louy liked to sprinkle her conversation with German words and phrases she was picking up from Lotta.

Herr Professor and Frau Alcott, Lotta decided, must be very important people in the city. Look how they had arranged for Karl to pay for the food he had stolen, and his fine, by working part of each day for the butcher and greengrocer he had robbed! In addition, these merchants were to "pay" Karl each day some still-good meat and vegetables they had been unable to sell. The Mullers would no longer go hungry, so long as Karl kept his part of the bargain.

"And maybe," Lotta thought, "Karl may have a *real* job with them later, if he behaves!" She didn't dare speak of that hope, even to Louy. She just hugged it to her heart.

Lotta didn't know what took place between Karl and Mutti on his return, for she did not witness the reunion. She was staying at Dedham Street, sleeping on the sofa in the book-filled drawing room. Frau Alcott insisted she stay with them until Mutti's fever broke. "It will make your mother rest easier, my dear, as you've done so much already. Where would your family be if *you* came down sick? I've had a word with that Mrs. Callaghan, and she'll see to it that your mother's all right." Frau Alcott also persuaded a doctor to call on the Mullers and not send a bill. Lotta, when she heard this, almost burst into tears. Instead, she hugged Frau Alcott hard. *"Liebe Frau,* you are guardian angel!"

"Funny angel in bonnet and shawl," Louy said, laughing.

Herr Professor was another guardian angel. At first she had been terrified of him. He was so tall, so thin, so stooped, with thin, pale hair straggling on either side of a high forehead and a large head. His light blue eyes either gazed vaguely into the distance or blazed with fire. His pockets were always stretched out of shape with books or apples. At the supper table that first night, while Frau Alcott was still out helping Karl, Herr Professor had fixed her with a piercing gaze and examined her closely on how she had learned to read and write.

"Father," Louy protested, laughing, "you're frightening the poor girl! Let her eat!"

"Show Lotta how you taught us our letters, Father," Lizzie urged.

Herr Professor uncoiled himself from his chair, bowed to Lotta, and sat down on the floor, his right side toward Lotta, his legs straight out in front together, and his arms glued to his sides.

"L," chorused Louy and Lizzie.

He stood straight up, one arm against his side and the other holding his stovepipe hat a foot above his head.

"I," chanted his two older daughters.

Down on the floor again, he contorted his body at a crazy angle, so that arms and legs pointed in opposite directions.

"Z," May joined in, giggling.

Another Z, another I, and a contorted E. By this time the image of that earlier, hated professor was blotted out of Lotta's mind, and Louy's father had become *the* Herr Professor. After he heard her read German aloud, he announced he would set out a reading program for her. "In German and in English. After you learn more English, perhaps you will help me with my German pronunciation. My friend Dr. Emerson tells me I would profit from some instruction." After that Lotta purely and simply loved him.

One thing Frau Alcott was unable to do was find Vater. At least Mutti didn't have to worry that Vater was in a hospital or jail, for Frau Alcott had checked those places. "That's a comfort to her, my dear," Frau Alcott told Lotta in her motherly fashion. "And her fever's going down, thanks to the good doctor who recognized her pneumonia and knew how to treat it. And to a good daughter who learned nursing skills from her dear mother and knew how and when to use them."

Lotta ducked her head, embarrassed. She had picked up a good deal more English since coming to Dedham Street, but she still felt uncomfortable at the ease with which the Alcotts expressed their feelings. "I must go back home now," she said.

"I think not quite yet, dear. Wait a few more days, until your mother's stronger. And you, also," Frau Alcott said gently. "There will be much for you to do at home, for your mother is still quite weak, and near her time. I will visit her daily, and tell you as soon as you may go."

That time came three days later, on a cold, bright morning. The wind and snow had stopped, and Boston had become a city of ice. The tree branches were sheathed in it, like blown-glass miniatures Lotta had seen at the Schloss. Sleighs drawn by prancing horses, bells jingling, dashed over the sheets of ice that were the roads. Lotta picked her way gingerly, holding her shawl tight around her. Her head and throat were wrapped in a gay muffler Lizzie had knitted for her. "I only had scraps of yarn, but they're cheerful," Lizzie apologized.

"They'll keep her warm," Louy said briskly, "and that's what matters." She thrust a pair of mittens at Lotta. "I burned a hole in one of 'em using it as a pot holder, I'm afraid. But they're better 'n nothing!" She hugged Lotta. "You remember your bargain, hear? I'll see you tomorrow!"

"If Mutti says," Lotta mumbled.

She couldn't say she didn't want to leave. Not when Mutti needed her, when she really *did* want to be with her own family! But the Alcott home was so *gemütlich*. That was one of Mutti's favorite words; it meant friendly, filled with warmth and love, cozy. Mutti knew how to make a home that way, but she didn't have the means. Not like the Alcotts clearly did!

Why did Vater have to get into trouble so we had to leave the Schloss? she thought bitterly.

Why did Vater desert them? That was the real question, wasn't it?

Lotta's face burned, from shame as well as cold. She started to run, trying to outrace her unkind thoughts, and fell on the ice in consequence.

Then she was in the lane, in the house, running up the stairs and seeing Michael's cheerful face pop around the Callaghans' door. "So yer back!" he called, grinning widely. "Sure, an' it's been quiet around here wi'out hearin' ye scold the bairns! Yer Karl's doin' right well, he's even civil to me when he sees me!"

Lotta just nodded, in a hurry to see her mother. Then the door to the Mullers' room opened and Tilda was standing there, thinner and paler, but her face alight. Hansi and Lena crowded behind her. And there was Mutti, in her chair, by the stove on which a soup kettle steamed. Her feet were propped on a rolled-up coverlet, she was very frail, and there seemed to be more gray in her soft hair, but she was Mutti.

Lotta ran into her arms.

Then she straightened, startled. "The baby *kicked* me!"

"*Ja*, he kicks a lot, this one. I am sure it is a boy because he is so strong." Mutti smiled. "Let me look at you, Daughter. Frau Alcott has taken good care of you, too. Your cheeks are rosier."

"It's the cold."

"And you have put on some weight. That is good. And you are wearing a new dress."

"Louy gave it to me. She's outgrown it."

"Louy?" Mutti looked puzzled. "A boy's name?"

"Louisa. She's sixteen. She's a writer. And Lizzie's—"

"Slowly, child," Mutti said, smiling, exactly as Frau Alcott often said to Louy. "Sit down beside me and tell me about these Alcotts."

Lotta sat on the floor beside the stove, her legs tucked under her. The words poured out breathlessly—about Louy, about the other girls, and Annie, their older sister, who was away as a governess and was going to open a school. About Frau Alcott, and Herr Professor, and all the books. She told Mutti about the bargain she had made with Louy, and Mutti nodded. "*Ja*, it is a good idea for you to learn so. And to help these kind friends who have done so much for us."

Except find Vater. The thought pushed its way into Lotta's mind like a twisting worm.

It wasn't until she was lying wakeful in the dark, with Tilda and Lena snuggled next to her on the mattress in the old way, that something else struck her.

No one had mentioned Vater. Not once. Not when she and Mutti were talking. Not when Karl came home, bringing sausage and potatoes and looking more at peace than Lotta had seen him look for some time. Not when they were all talking together as Lotta, with Tilda's help, assembled dinner. Not even—this was most shocking of all—when Mutti said the prayer before the meal. It was as if everyone, herself included, was afraid to mention him. Or as if they had forgotten him as completely as he, apparently, had forgotten them.

As February tightened its grip on Boston, Lotta led two lives. One was at home, where Mutti was waiting out the last weeks until the baby came. Frau Alcott brought a basket of baby garments, somewhat worn but beautifully washed and ironed, and she also gave Mutti a bundle of remnants, muslin and flannel. Mutti cut out little nightgowns, petticoats, and wrappers, and she and Lotta sewed on them while they talked, or while Mutti took the younger children through their lessons.

Mutti had learned about Lotta's keeping the lesson up, because Hansi had bragged about his progress, and she had been impressed. "You should continue with the teaching, Daughter. It will help you, also."

"You can do it better," Lotta said gruffly. She could not tell Mutti her real reason, which was that the only book they had to read from was the Bible. There was too much about God the Father in the daily lessons, and Lotta had had more than she could stomach of thinking about either God or fathers.

Her other life was at the Alcotts', where everything was so beautiful and spacious. Lotta spent part of each day there, and mostly she and Louy were alone together. Lizzie and May went to a small school run by a Miss Peabody, who was a friend of Herr Professor's. Herr Professor was out most of the time, conducting his "conversations" or visiting friends. Frau Alcott had set up what she called a Mission to the Poor in a storefront on Washington Street. She came home full of stories about people in trouble as Karl had been, people newly "off the boat" with nowhere to live, families like the Callaghans with ten or twelve children, sometimes in a single room.

"In a way, you are fortunate, my dear, having a nice *big* room. And your mother has divided it so cleverly."

Lotta didn't remind her that after the baby was born there would be eight in that one room. *If* Vater came home. How could kindly Frau Alcott, with four rooms for five people, understand?

She was spending more time at the Alcotts' than she should, Lotta knew, but no one told her not to. It was so peaceful. Her English was improving. There wasn't really much work for her to do there. With only Louy home most of the time, the place didn't get very dirty—not like the Mullers' building did, at any rate. The food Louy cooked was sparse and simple, with not many pots and pans to rattle. A good part of the time Lotta roamed through Herr Professor's wonderful library or read by the fire while Louy wrote. Sometimes Louy read bits of her stories aloud or acted out parts Lotta couldn't understand. Louy, Lotta found, liked to use very fancy words in her stories, and the tales were peppered with dangerous villains, swooning maidens, and golden-haired heroes. Most of the stories were laid in castles with convenient dungeons.

"Vy you write about dose places, not America?" Lotta asked. She was still having trouble pronouncing English *w*'s and *th*'s.

Louy ran her fingers through her hair, causing her thick chestnut-colored braids to cascade down. She stretched grandly. "Because they're so romantic. And exciting. All the knights and princesses and titled noblemen and everything. Did you ever meet any titled noblemen, Lotta?"

Lotta didn't answer. She kept her eyes on the little frock she was sewing for Johannes or Johanna, and to her relief, Louy didn't repeat the question.

By the time Frau Alcott returned, Lotta had finished blind-sewing the seams and was putting rows of tiny tucks along the bottom. Frau Alcott examined it closely and smiled at Lotta.

"My dear, you sew beautifully! Such tiny, even stitches! Who taught you?"

"Mutti," Lotta replied, flushing with pleasure.

"You are a fortunate young lady. With a skill like that, you will always be able to earn money. I hope a sewing machine will never be invented, for it would put scores of honest women out of well-paying work."

"*I* say one should be invented, the sooner the better, and women should man 'em, and make a lot more money because the work would go faster!" Louy jabbed her needle through the sheet she was hemming.

"Of course they should, but I see scant chance of women being offered work in factories," Frau Alcott said briskly. "Although I do hear girls are working in the glove factories in Seneca Falls. But how much better to be able to work at home and look after one's own family at the same time. I must speak to your mother about taking in sewing after the baby's born," she added, smiling at Lotta. "There will never be a machine made that will hem as well as a woman's fingers."

At first Lotta thought the Alcott girls were sewing for their own family or for their marriage chests. But then she realized they were speaking about "the sheets for Aunt Robie" and "the handkerchiefs for Cousin Willis." She didn't dare ask Frau Alcott, but she did ask Louy. The beginning of an idea had begun to shape itself in Lotta's mind.

"Marmee's had us sewing for our bread and apples ever since we could hold a needle," Louy said. "She thinks it's one of the most important skills a woman can learn. It's certainly come in handy! Lizzie could sew beautifully when she was only five. Marmee and Annie are the best, of course, and May will do well once she learns patience, because she loves pretty things. I don't mind sewing, 'cause my mind can run off on story plots while I'm running up seams. But *I'll* never win a prize for tiny, even stitches!" She yanked her needle through the heavy muslin sheet.

"Vy you sew, den?" Lotta asked bluntly.

"For the Alcott Sinking Fund," Louy answered frankly. She pointed to a covered bean pot on an upper shelf. "Don't tell May, because she might raid it for things like pickled limes or a new hair ribbon. It's the pin money we Alcott women put away for the catastrophes that are sure to come."

They stopped to look up "catastrophe" in the German-English dictionary.

"Marmee believes every woman, rich or poor, should develop her talents—whether for sewing, or cooking, or teaching, or nursing. Or writing books, or painting pictures! She says even the richest woman can never be sure a catastrophe won't happen. Look at Grandfather May! *He* was very wealthy." Louy's eyes were dreamy. "I remember him as an old man, still wearing black velvet kneebreeches with jeweled buckles, and silver shoebuckles. But he backed a friend's business, and when the friend couldn't make good on the bills, Granfather May had to. It was a debt of honor. After that Grandfather May was still *comfortable,* but not rich anymore."

It was like one of Louy's own tales, Lotta thought, enthralled. "Vat happen den?" she asked.

"What? Oh, he died when I was small," Louy answered. "Did you know, Lotta, that until last year no woman could inherit anything, not even from her husband or her father? It always had to be left to her husband, her brother, or her son, to 'handle' for her! Suppose they *mishandle* it? That's why Marmee says every woman must be prepared to look out for herself and for her children."

Like we'll have to do if Vater doesn't come home, Lotta thought. And then it struck her. *No. Not "if." Like we're doing already.*

Chapter Eight

February 1849

T he blizzards returned, three in one week, shrouding the city in a cold, suffocating blanket. *I hate winter,* Lotta thought savagely, trying to wrap herself in the coverlet without leaving Tilda or Lena exposed to the chill night air.

Winters in Germany had been as cold, but everything had been different there. Their house was warmer, and *clean.* In the Mullers' room it was impossible to wash and dry oneself or one's clothes properly. Mostly they wore everything as long as possible rather than have to put them on damp and risk further illness. In Germany it had been possible to run and jump in the snowy fields without falling painfully on icy walks. The children had been able to ride atop the sledges dragging great logs from the forest to the Schloss and its workers' homes. And once every year, just before Lent began, there had been a winter carnival on the Schloss's grounds. Not last year, of course—

Lotta shut away the memory of last year firmly. None of the Mullers spoke of it, any more than they spoke now of Vater.

With the snow so deep, Mutti didn't let the younger children go out unless the sun shone and Karl or Lotta was with them. But the sun shone seldom, and Karl was seldom home. "I'm working, remember?" he said curtly, when anyone brought up the subject. The result was that the inside dampness—and fumes from the stove—didn't improve either their health or their dispositions. But at least they had food.

"We must be grateful for what God sends," Mutti said.

"God or Frau Alcott?" Lotta demanded, shoveling in some of their small supply of coal. The stove had a voracious appetite.

"*Ja*, she is our Frau Greatheart, but it is God in her heart who sends her."

Lotta slammed the stove door and turned away, biting back the retort that would have shocked and grieved Mutti.

Cooped up in the room, Hansi was becoming a handful. He didn't see why he should study, since Karl didn't. "Men don't have to!" He had Mutti's reluctant permission to play on the landing with the two youngest Callaghan boys, both older than he, but they didn't stay there. The three of them rampaged noisily through the building, from the damp cellar where bleary-eyed old Peg-Leg Jackson had a room, to the attic, which was half storage space and half the room of two burly seaman brothers. Lotta knew, but she didn't dare risk upsetting Mutti, and Hansi wouldn't listen to *her*. Twice he escaped the building completely and went rampaging with the Callaghan boys. Once he came home alone; once Michael returned him, looking grim.

"He's gittin' inter places yer ma wouldn't want him," he told Lotta.

"He vas vit *your* brothers!" Lotta flared. "I cannot vatch him all de time!"

"Nah, yer too busy trottin' over ter yer foine friends, aint-cha?" Michael retorted sarcastically, and turned his back to open his own door.

"*Michael Callaghan—*"

The Callaghan door banged shut in Lotta's face. From below in the stairwell came the sound of other doors closing. Lotta, scarlet with fury and embarrassment, turned on Hansi with a low-voiced scolding that had no effect. The next afternoon he was gone again, and worst of all, Lotta didn't know it until Karl came home from the Market, dragging a screaming Hansi behind him.

The sounds penetrated the building from cellar to attic from the moment Karl and his captive burst through the front door. Lotta flew out to the landing, shutting the Muller door behind her, hearing doors opening on all the other floors as she did so. "Hush!" she ordered in a harsh whisper. "Mutti's sleeping."

To her relief, her brothers looked at each other and grew quiet.

"Get inside! And not a weep nor a whimper from you in front of Mutti!" Karl commanded in a low voice. Hansi scuttled inside without a word, leaving Karl and Lotta to face each other.

"What was that all about?" Lotta asked.

"Don't you *know?*" Karl retorted. "I found Hansi in the Market, darting around between the horses, trying to pick up coppers in the gutter! Why did you let him go down there alone?"

"I didn't! I thought he was playing here on the landing with the Callaghans."

"Well, he wasn't. And he could have been killed!"

"You know so much about the dangers in the Market, *you* talk to him!" Lotta snapped, shaken.

"Can't you take some of the responsibility?" Karl demanded, his voice rising. "I'm out working!"

"So am I!"

"Helping the gentry," Karl jeered. "Forgetting everything we've learned about how much *that* kind can be relied on!"

"The Alcotts aren't like that!"

"Then why aren't you getting paid?"

"I *am!* In English lessons . . . and reading!"

"Fat lot of good that'll do you!" Karl snorted.

"You need to speak English in this country in order to get work! You need to read and write to get anywhere! Oh, yes, *you're* working without it," Lotta swept on, as Karl purpled with fury. "We all know how and why you got *your* job! They're only paying you in food because they feel sorry for us!"

"At least you're eating!" Karl shouted. "So from now on, you stay home and look after things here so I *can* work!"

"Who made you head of the family?"

"I have to be, since Vater deserted us!"

For an instant they just stared at each other. Then Lotta, to her shock, burst into tears.

In the stillness that followed, the squeaks of doors being closed drifted up the stairs.

Karl put an arm around Lotta and patted her shoulder awkwardly. *"Ach, Lottchen,"* he said gruffly, using Vater's name for her. "I'm sorry."

Lotta wiped her eyes on her sleeve. "It's just . . . nobody *mentions* him. It's as though he's dead."

"Maybe he is," Karl said after a moment, soberly. "Your fine Alcotts haven't managed to find him, have they? If they ever tried."

Karl talked to Hansi about the dangers of the Market, and Hansi's responsibility to look after his sisters at home when Karl wasn't there. Lotta kept going to the Alcotts'.

The place was Lotta's refuge, but after that day, in some incalculable way, some of the glow was gone. Maybe it was the things she and Karl had said. Maybe it was just winter, which was taking its toll on the Alcott household, too. Louy came down with a bad cold, which did not improve her disposition. She spent a good deal of time under an old afghan on the couch, wiping her red nose and writing, and her voice was hoarse. Lizzie took over the cooking and the sewing, with Lotta's help. May was supposed to be helping, too, but she usually found reason not to, to Lotta's irritation. The relationship between May and Lotta was sometimes like that between two spitting cats.

It wasn't that Lotta disliked May—she thought May very pretty, and her fine airs mostly funny. It wasn't that May disliked Lotta—"she doesn't know me well enough for that," Lotta thought—or that she was jealous because Lotta and Louy were what Louy called "kindred souls." Lotta knew by now that it was Annie, the absent older sister, who was May's "other mother." It was Lizzie who was Louy's pet, and gentle Lizzie didn't have a jealous bone in her body. It was the way May *patronized* her that Lotta resented.

"And she's four years younger than I am," Lotta thought, irked.

Things came to a head on an afternoon late in February. Snow had turned to sleet that beat relentlessly against the windowpanes and came down the chimney, sputtering against logs in the small fire that burned on the Alcott hearth. May had caught Louy's cold and been forced to stay home from a coveted invitation to take tea at the home of one of Frau Alcott's cousins. Louy was at home for the same reason. Louy also had a splitting headache, and a sheet to finish hemming, and a fit of literary inspiration that had seized her aching brain. Between sneezes, she was dashing back and forth between the sheet spread over the table and her papers, pen, and inkpot sitting on the drainboard of the sink.

"Tarnation! Now I've knocked over the inkpot," she cried despairingly, watching a rivulet of black run across her pages and drip onto the floor. She stooped to pick the pot up, trailing her hem in the ink and giving a prodigious sneeze. The papers went flying.

Lizzie ran to scoop the sheet out of danger.

"I'll clean the ink," Lotta said, looking around for mop, rags, or scrub brush.

"No need for you to get inky because of my carelessness," Louy said curtly.

"Louy's altogether too careless," May said, obviously quoting somebody else. "Her head's always in her stories, instead of on *fastiduous* things."

"If you can't pronounce 'fastidious' right, don't use the word," Louy snapped.

May wrinkled her nose. "At least *I* keep my clothes nice, instead of getting them all stained or burning my skirts against the stove, as you do. Mrs. Gardiner told Aunt Sewall I'm a perfect little lady."

"I'll 'perfect little lady' you if you don't stop being Miss Hoity-Toity," Louy retorted. "And don't talk like that before guests. You're embarrassing Lotta."

"Lotta's not a guest," May sniffed. "She's 'help.' The aunts say Marmee's carrying charity too far, taking shiftless foreigners into her home when everybody knows they're not even clean! And who knows what germs they're bringing in?"

"Hold your tongue!"

"Abbie May!"

Louy and Lizzie both spoke together. Louy's eyes were furious. Rage surged through Lotta. She clenched her fists and willed it down until she could stop her jaw from trembling. "I can finish hemming the sheet for you, Louy," she said in a low voice.

"I wouldn't let her," May said importantly. "*She's* not clean, either. Her skin's all gray where it's not red from cold. So are her petticoats, and her dress looks like it's been slept in."

Lotta whirled on her. "You'd be dirty, too, Fraulein Abbie May Alcott, if you didn't live in a fine home like this! If you hadn't enough coal to heat wash water because there was scarcely enough for cooking! *If* you had anything to cook! *Ja*, sometimes we sleep in our clothes because the room's so cold! And when we *do* wash clothes or sheets, they won't dry! That's probably how Mutti got pneumonia!"

Lizzie gave a small gasp. Louy tried to interrupt. Lotta swung around.

"You teach me English, *und* I help you clean, because ve made a bargain, *ja*? I am not a serf! I help vit other t'ings because I vant to. *Und* I sew *good*, Frau Alcott said so!" Lotta's English grammar was slipping away from her in her shame and fury. "I vouldn't ruin your sheet! I touch your books no more if I might get dem dirty!" Her eyes were welling with tears and she pushed them back with her fist, leaving inky streaks. "I t'ought ve vere friends! I am sorry if I vas wrong!"

"We *are* friends," Louy said gruffly, reaching out her arm.

Lotta dashed it away, the red rage engulfing her. "You cannot understand vat dese *shiftless foreigners* dat come to your so-cold city of freedom haf go—gone—t'rough! *Mein Vater*—he *gutt* man—nobody gif him vork. You t'ink you understand, but you do not." She turned on May, who shrank back in shock into Lizzie's arms. "You t'ink you are fine lady? You t'ink you a princess? I haf met princess, *und* she not act like you! You never been hungry! You never been sick *und* haf no doctor! You never not haf roof over head, or place to sleep. Is easy to keep clean *und* act like lady ven you live in fine home like dis, beautiful t'ings, never afraid, never go to bed hungry—"

"*That's enough!*" Louy clapped her hands over her ears. Her eyes were blazing. "You call this place fine? I'll tell you what's fine! Grandmother May's silver teapot that Marmee had to sell when her toes were quite out of her shoes, and the charity bundle sent us had no clothes in it for Baby May! When we ate only bread and water for meals, when the apples ran out, except for a real treat of potatoes and squash for Thanksgiving dinner!"

Lotta's stunned voice came in a thin, high whisper. "Vat is T'anksgiving?"

Louy just swept on. "Do you think we don't know what it's like to be so poor and hungry you think there's 'most no hope left, and you're scared of the family being broken up for good? To be scared your father's going to just give up and die? To be so cold when the wind comes whistling through cracks in the walls that even huddled up four in a bed you can't stop shivering—and you get a cough that makes your sides ache and won't go away—and you can hear your father and mother fighting—and your mother crying? To think you may never see your father again?"

"Louisa, don't," Lizzie said in a whisper.

"So don't try telling *us* we don't understand!" Louy banged her inkpot down onto the table so hard that the remaining ink leapt out of it. *"You have no idea!"*

In the stunned silence that followed, Lotta's thin whisper came again. "At least nobody try to kill your father."

Again, silence. Lotta felt Lizzie's arm go around her waist, and Lizzie pressed a handkerchief into her hand. Louy was just staring at her. May rose, unnaturally subdued. "I think I'll go get in bed," she said in a muted voice, and disappeared. Lizzie followed.

Lotta had begun to shake, worse than during the scene with Karl, worse than ever. She shook and shook as a hollow coldness gripped her, until she was bent double with the pain of her sobs. Her arms locked across her waist as though she were trying to hold herself together.

"What happened?" Louy asked gently.

When her teeth stopped chattering, Lotta wiped her eyes on Lizzie's handkerchief with its crocheted edge.

"We live—lived—at Schloss von Reisenthal," she said carefully. "Not in big house. Small house, but very beautiful . . . flowers growing on roof. Mutti vas pastor's daughter. Vater . . . Vater's father in army, saved life of Captain von Reisenthal, and de baron very grateful. Even after de captain later killed. The baron gif—gave—Grossmutter Muller *gut* job, *und* Vater grow up at Schloss. He *loved* it dere . . ."

Lotta stopped until her voice steadied while Louy waited in silence. "Vater haf to go into army very young," she went on at last. "Ven he come back, baron gif him job, *und* ven Vater and Mutti marry, he gif dem house to live in. But after baron die—" Lotta swallowed, and winked back tears. "Everyt'ing change."

"How?" Louy asked. When Lotta just shook her head, not speaking, she went on. "I don't mean to pry, truly. But you might feel less . . . homesick if you talked about it. I always feel better if I talk to Marmee, or to Father. Or if I write. I keep a journal, and Marmee knows she's always free to read it. Sometimes she writes me little notes in it, and they help a lot."

Lotta shook her head again. "To speak of dis to Mutti or to Vater . . . it gif dem too much pain."

"You could talk to Marmee. Or to me. I'm a good listener," Louy said, "and I can keep secrets, truly I can." She stopped, reddening. "I'm sorry. It's none of my business."

"Is no secret," Lotta said at last. "Baron's nephew inherit title and Schloss, and t'ings very different . . ."

"How?" Louy asked, not moving.

Lotta shrugged. "Last year, two years, troubles everywhere in Europe. Famines. Revolutions. Peasants abused. *Ve* not peasants, but Vater see wrongs happening, and he grow—grew—angry. He . . . joined a group of his friends, former soldiers . . . to make t'ings better."

"Revolutionaries?" Louy asked quietly.

Lotta nodded, not looking up. "Den t'ings get worse, *und* dey get discouraged. Vater's friend Herr Weiss, he haf heard dere is vork dey can do, vork dey are good at, in America. Herr Weiss come ahead; he is single man, no children. It take Vater longer to save money."

A log broke in the fire. Louy waited for Lotta to continue. There was a faint rustle in the doorway. Lizzie had returned and stood there, quietly listening. Lotta swallowed hard. "In the night comes vord . . . soldiers vill be coming for Vater to arrest him. Vater must leave, quick, quick, in the night, vit'out us. He go to Hamburg, find work, use different name. Ve vait for him to send for us. Finally—" She lifted a hand, then let it fall. "Ve come here. No Herr Weiss vaiting. No job for Vater. Money all gone. *Und* now again, no Vater. But ve are *not shiftless!*"

She squeezed her eyes shut to hold back the tears.

Louy cleared her throat. "I had no idea things were so bad in Europe. I'd heard of the revolutions. Father's talked of them, and so has Mr. Emerson, our friend. I've read Goethe. And

Marmee's talked about the problems immigrants are having here. But I didn't *realize*—" She crossed the room to take Lotta's hands and squeeze them hard. "I'm so sorry for what May said, for what anybody else may have said to you," she said gruffly. "I wish there were something more we could do. I wish we could find your father. My parents have tried, truly they have. I guess we'll just have to leave it up to God to bring him back."

Lotta shook her head. "I not believe in dat anymore."

"One thing we can do," came Lizzie's voice from the doorway, "is let Lotta have a bath here, right now. And wash her clothes. We have enough coal to heat the water, and coal to dry them."

The bath was heavenly, in a real tin bathtub before the fire. Louy heated great kettles of water on the stove and poured them in, and while Lotta soaked her clothes soaked, too, in the Alcott washtub. Lizzie kept May out of the room, to Lotta's relief. Louy knelt by the tub and washed Lotta's hair for her and scrubbed her back. She could use, she discovered, a good deal of scrubbing. Afterward, wrapped in towels warmed before the fire, she sat in Marmee's chair and drank hot cider while her clothes dried. Louy even heated flatirons on the stove and ironed them.

"I want to tell you something, Lotta," Louy said presently, her back to Lotta. "I've never told anyone else, excepting Marmee. When I was your age, we moved into a funny old house in a town called Concord. It was right after that terrible time I just talked about. The house was nearly falling down, but Father had great plans for it. He added on rooms, doing all the work himself. I was to have a room all to myself for the first time, opening onto the lawn, the garden Father was making, and the forest. The room wouldn't be ready till spring, but in autumn, shortly before my thirteenth birthday, I woke at dawn one day and crept outside for a run in the woods. The dew was still on the moss, and the trees arching over my head were red and gold. Everything was so bright and beautiful

I couldn't keep from singing. Then the sun broke through the trees, flooding the meadows with a glorious light . . . for me alone to see. And I *felt* God, so close . . . I prayed to keep that sense of closeness always, and I have. It will happen for you, Lotta, somehow, in some way, if you'll let it."

Lotta didn't answer.

"Anyway," Louisa went on more briskly, "I got a room of my own in spring, and my stars! Do I wish I still had it! I will again one day. I made a plan for my life that spring, and I stick to it. I suppose folks would laugh over a girl of thirteen making a plan for her life, but I was old for my age, as you are. I'm going to be a writer, and I'm going to see that we're all safe, and never homeless or hungry again. I mean to make a quiet room for Marmee, where she can sit among beautiful things, and read good books, and visit with all sorts of pleasant people, and never have to work hard again."

"You think you can do this?" Lotta asked humbly.

"I *know* I can! I'll do any good and honest work I have to to make it happen. You can, too, Lotta, if you find your plan, and sort out what really matters, what's right for *you*. Father says if a man's right in his heart, and has intelligence and good health, all things are possible for him. I guess that's true for a woman also, no matter how little!"

Lotta cleared her throat. "I vill be thirteen in April. And I am not a child, either."

"Then you can make a plan for yourself, too, can't you?" Louy finished ironing Lotta's dress and draped it over a chair before the fire to air. "*You* watch it," she said. "May's too right about how I let things burn." Her eyes began to sparkle. "Your thirteenth birthday? I know! We'll make a real Alcott birthday celebration for you!"

"What is that?" Lotta asked.

Louy smiled tantalizingly. "Wait and see!"

Chapter Nine

February–March 1849

After that day, Lotta found she was watching the Alcotts with new eyes. Bit by bit she began to notice things or to see meaning in things she had noticed earlier and not understood— the sewing the Alcotts were always doing, even little May, and the Alcott Sinking Fund! The fact that Herr Professor, for all his wisdom, no longer had a school to teach in—nor, apparently, an income. It was the *women* who were paying the bills in the Alcott household. That would have shamed Vater, Lotta thought. But at the same time, she realized that the Alcotts, unlike the Mullers, always had food to eat—even though, from what Louy had said, that had not always been the case. She wondered what the story was behind that, but wouldn't ask. There were still Muller secrets she had no intention of ever telling, either.

She also noticed the great pride Herr Professor took in his womenfolk's accomplishments and the pride they had in his wisdom, though he was not the family provider. *They have respect for each other*, Lotta thought. Respect was a commodity that had been oozing away in the Muller household, hadn't it? Was that why Vater had gone, because he felt he could not face them? Was that why she and Karl always felt so angry?

Louy's right, Lotta thought. *I have to make a plan for my life if I want it to amount to something.* But she couldn't think any further just yet than getting through when the baby was born.

After that, after Mutti was back on her feet, she would ask Louy how *she* could earn some money. All The Alcotts were so sure about their talents, she thought enviously. Lotta had no idea what her own were, and she was not about to wait for God to show her.

The clothes for the baby were almost finished. Lotta, spurred by the Alcotts' example, had taught Tilda how to make button-holes and hems, and Lena how to do gathering and basting. If Lizzie could do those things at four, then so could Lena. Tilda and Mutti had also been knitting little stockings, caps, and wrappers.

One night Karl brought home a sturdy fruit basket from the Market. "For the baby," he said gruffly. "Gus was going to throw it out." Gus was the greengrocer he was working for.

"Show more respect," Mutti reproved. "You should not call the man by his first name."

"He told me to. When you work in the Market, you have to be able to call each other by something short and quick," Karl said calmly. "He says I have it in me to be a good Market man."

Mutti frowned. "You have no higher ambition?"

"It's putting food on the table, isn't it? That's enough for now."

Mutti, to Lotta's surprise, let that pass.

As the weather grew colder, time seemed to go more slowly. Partly because March would bring the baby, for which they now waited anxiously. Partly because Lotta had started thinking about Vater again, and worrying.

Was he alive?

Would he ever come back?

Maybe it would be better if he didn't . . .

It was at that point, always, that Lotta slammed the door firmly on her treacherous thoughts. But she was finding it harder and harder not to lose her temper. It was either that or cry. Lotta hated crying.

She hated apologizing, too, but she owed Louy one for exploding at her that unforgettable afternoon. It took a little while for her to make it. She didn't want to get into the subject in front of Herr Professor, or Frau Alcott, or even more especially, May. At last she found Louy alone. It was the first of March, a cold, bright morning. She stumbled through her rehearsed apology, and Louy told her not to worry.

"I owe you an apology, too, remember? So let's shake hands on it like two gentlemen and then forget it. I lose my temper often enough, heaven knows. Although I do think I'm getting better. The cork just popped when you touched a few raw spots that day. I'm vain enough to think I'm learning to hold my temper, but I wonder if I'll ever be able to hold my tongue!"

"*Bitte?* How did you learn to hold your temper?" Lotta asked.

Louy laughed ruefully. "A lot of pinching myself until I'm black and blue! No, truly, it's partly from talking with Marmee and coming to learn how she's had her own silent battle with temper all these years. And partly from seeing how truly noble Father's been, how patiently he's borne disappointments and discouragements. His disappointments put my petty ones to shame." She was silent for a moment, then began scrubbing a crusted frying pan vigorously. "That's another of the things I mean to do when I'm rich and famous, give Father his one perfect school at last!"

"Vhy does Herr Professor not teach in real school anymore? Is it all right I ask?"

"It's all right. Just don't do it in front of him. It's because Father respects children, really respects them, more than most people do, including their own parents. Because he believes in telling the truth about everything, even to children. And because he's too wise and learned for most people to understand what he's saying, and what they do understand frightens a lot of them." Louy set the cleaned frying pan aside and attacked a large iron kettle. "Oh, Lotta, you should have seen the school he had once upstairs in the Masonic Temple on Temple Place. A desk for every child—Father made them himself—and each with its own bookcase. Fine pictures on the walls, and maps, and busts of great writers and philosophers! And Miss Peabody's velvet sofa to curl up on to read. Father used to garland the walls with evergreens, and bring in fresh flowers, for study and for beauty. And the children were learning so well."

"What happened?" Lotta asked involuntarily.

"Father taught things the parents didn't approve," Louy said shortly. "But *they* were the ones who were wrong, not he. After a while he had another school, and it was doing well, and do you know what happened? He admitted a girl named Susan Robinson, a nice, intelligent girl, and all the families but one promptly withdrew their children. And do you know why?"

Lotta shook her head.

"Because Susan was black. A Negro, a person of the African race," Louisa elaborated, when Lotta looked blank. "Almost everyone in Boston's opposed to slavery, but they don't want their children to study with anyone who isn't white! Or of their own particular church, probably, if it came to that."

Lotta's knowledge of English, and of America, wasn't up to this. She looked at Louy blankly. Louy laughed and hung her damp dishcloth before the stove to dry, and sat down on the three-legged cricket by the fire. "Don't worry about it. You're learning about America, warts and all, fast enough. Just try to hold your tongue, if you can't hold your temper. Go outside and throw snowballs against the wall to work that off. I don't blame you for getting angry, Lotta. Father says there are a lot of things in life we *should* get angry over. But then we have to pick ourselves up by our bootstraps and make things better *ourselves!* Women can, you know, if we try. Look at Marmee. Look at my sister Annie, out teaching, and all of us sewing. Everybody's got something that's theirs to do, and if they've got brains and energy, they can just do it!"

Lotta frowned. "Like your writing?"

Louisa nodded. "Like my writing. That's my *special* thing. Only I haven't sold any stories—yet—so in the meantime there's teaching, and sewing. And nursing. I like nursing. You figure out what you're good at, Lottchen, and you do it. Don't let anybody talk you out of trying." She grinned. "And if you need to swear a little first, that's all right, too."

"What is swearing?"

"Like you heard me do that afternoon. *'Christopher Columbus!'* " Louy grinned again. "That's not real swearing, it's what I say instead of the real bad words so I won't get skinned alive. Now you try it."

"Christopher Columbus!"

"That's it. And think of all the nasty, mean things you want to say, and let 'em out while you say, 'Great galloping geraniums!' "

"Great galloping geraniums!" Lotta bellowed. She took a deep breath and smiled. Louy winked and went to check the apple cake in the oven.

There was a tap at the door.

"Get that, will you, Lotta?" Louy called over her shoulder.

Before Lotta could reach the door, it opened.

"Who are you teaching your dreadful slang to, Louisa?" a pretty young woman called.

"Annie!" Louy dropped her pot holder and ran to the newcomer. "Why didn't you let us know you were coming?"

"Didn't know till this morning. Uncle Bond had to come into town to do some business, so Aunt suggested I come along, attend to some shopping errands for her, and stay the night with you all. I'm to return by the morning train. Where's Marmee?"

"Down at the relief office, and Father's off somewhere talking. With luck, they'll be home in time for supper." Louy held her sister off. "Look at you, with real lace collar and cuffs and a rose in your bonnet!"

Annie pirouetted for Louy's benefit, her crinoline rustling. "The collar and cuffs are a gift from Aunt Bond, and the rose is off her new bonnet. She thought the color didn't suit her complexion. I wished I had you to sew it on for me. You always have such a flair for style."

"When it comes to other folks' clothes, you mean?" Louy countered. "Thanks, I'll turn myself into a fashion plate when I can afford a real silk dress, but until then I'll stick to comfort and leave the fine airs to you and May." She shook her head ruefully. "I might have known you'd turn into a lady, grown the minute I let you out of my sight!"

"Marmee says it's kindness and good manners that make the lady, not birth or dress. And as for growing up, I've been a working woman for two years now. Longer, if you count the sewing we've done at home."

"Oh, I do, every stitch and penny." Louy grimaced. "So that makes me a worker all right, but I'm blessed if I'll submit to being labeled a grown-up lady till I'm rich and famous from my writing. Then it'll be silk dresses all round, and a velvet-collared greatcoat for Father, and I'll do the social round for the good of my books. Rather stick to being Sairy Gamp in a garret any day. Remember what fun we had, Annie, playing *Pilgrim's Progress* at Hillside?"

"Do I? Pulling ourselves out of the Slough of Despond, and breaking out of the Iron Cage of Despair, climbing the hill of the attic stairs with Marmee's ragbags tied on our backs for burdens, till we reached the top and they all fell off and went rolling down—"

"—into the scrub pail and got soaking wet, the time we played in the house because it was raining, and Marmee wasn't pleased."

Annie chuckled. "That was nothing like the time you decided we should use that swampy spot out back for a *real* slough, and came into the house dripping mud and pond litter. My stars, how Marmee's May temperament exploded that day, till Father calmed her." She was silent for a moment. "Ah, well, we may have lost sight of the Delectable Mountains at times, but we're living in Marmee's Celestial City again, aren't we?"

"Don't start me on that," Louy said darkly. Then she laughed and pulled Lotta forward. "Miss Alcott, may I present my own private and particular prize pilgrim, Fraulein Carlotta Muller? Lotta, this is my older sister, Anna Bronson Alcott."

Annie turned to Lotta with a warm smile. "So *you're* the new pilgrim whose progress Louisa's been writing me about so often! I'm so glad to meet you!"

"*Bitte?*" Lotta asked, puzzled. "Vat is pilgrim? Progress?"

"*Pilgrim's Progress* is Father's favorite book."

"It's a game we used to play."

Both sisters answered at once. Then they took turns explaining that the pilgrim in the story was like the immigrants who had colonized Massachusetts, fleeing from a troubled old life in search of a better new one, both real in their hearts.

"Like Vater." The words escaped from Lotta before she knew they were coming. She turned her head away quickly, but not before she saw Annie and Louy exchange glances.

"Like all of you Mullers," Louy said firmly. "Like our Alcott ancestors, if you come down to it. *They* were among the original Boston Puritans. Over a hundred years ago our great-great-grandfather moved down into Connecticut and started a farm called Spindle Hill. He grew flax to be woven into linen cloth. By the time Father was born, times were hard and very little of the farm remained. But it's still there. Grandmother Alcott could scarcely read or write, but she taught Father his letters by drawing them with a stick in the sand on the floor. And she made sure Father went to school. She kept a journal, so when Father was a boy he started keeping one, too. You should, too, Lotta. So many exciting things have happened to you! And it would be good practice for your English."

Lotta shook her head. "I do not have book. Anyway—"

"Anyway *what?*"

"Nothing."

"*Now* who's being as nosy as our youngest sister?" Annie asked innocently.

Louy laughed sheepishly. "It's my author's instinct. You don't need a real journal, Lotta. Father made his first one by sewing together bits of paper. He whittled a goose quill for a pen and mixed soot and vinegar for ink."

"You should see his journals now," Annie chuckled. "Thousands of pages."

Lotta frowned, trying to puzzle out the meaning of unfamiliar words. "A book? Like *Pilgrim's Progress?*"

"Good for you, Lotta!" Louy's eyes sparkled.

"Father says that's what everyone's life is," Annie added. "Filled with all sorts of good and bad events, within and without, but with the promise of better to come if we're 'strong for the right.' " She glanced slyly at her sister. "Has Louy told you about her idol, Mr. Emerson? He says everyone has it in him to be a hero or heroine. Perhaps not the great spectacular kind, like poets and philosophers and military leaders. But with the kind of quiet bravery that perseveres through all adversity and never loses faith."

"Like Herr Professor and the Temple School?"

Annie swung around. "Oh, Louy! What have you been telling her?"

"Nothing I shouldn't. Only how brave and splendid Father was," Louy said hastily. "If you want an example of a quiet hero, Lotta, look at Marmee. Or at your mother."

Lotta nodded mutely, her eyes filling.

"I think Carlotta understands," Annie said gently. "For heaven's sake, tell us something cheerful, Louy, before we dissolve in floods of sentiment. What are you writing now?"

Louy grinned wickedly. "A very cheerful story! A kidnapped maiden, at least one murder, and a treasure buried in a crypt beneath a castle. Is a Schloss the same thing as a castle, Lotta? Annie, this mean girl knew a real live baron and a princess, and she won't tell me anything about them! Maybe I can put you in my story, Lotta. Or your father. What did he do in Germany? His work, I mean, after he was in the army?"

"He trained and took care of horses," Lotta said carefully. "For drills and racing."

"Christopher Columbus!" Louy said in wonder. "What made your father think he could find work like that in Boston?"

Lotta shook her head. "Not Boston. Virginia. He not know Boston and Virginia so far apart. Boat fare to Boston cheaper."

"No wonder—" Louy started to say, and stopped. Lotta swallowed.

"No vonder he not find vork in Boston? Ve know now. But ve always live in country. Not know about cities."

Louy and Anna exchanged glances. Then Annie rose in a swish of petticoats. "Mercy me, it must be lunchtime, and I'm quite famished. What's the state of the Alcott larder, Louy? I'll set the table."

"Split-pea soup and apple cake, fresh this morning. Served with a flourish in a minute, your ladyship. But first I have something else to tend to." Louy opened a cupboard and reached to the top shelf. Then she went to Lotta, a thin book with marbled covers pressed in her arms.

"Here you are, Fraulein Muller. It's the book I was saving to write my next story in, so don't say I've never made a noble sacrifice. Take it for your journal."

Chapter Ten

March 1849

Lotta wrote in her journal regularly, and wrote in English whenever she knew the right words. That way, if Karl or Tilda found it, they couldn't read it. She slept with it under her pillow and carried it with her when she left the house, just in case. For Louy had been right, Lotta found. Confiding things to a journal, or working them through on paper, *did* help.

A few days after Lotta's talk with Louy and Annie, Herr Professor came home early in the afternoon and asked Lotta to come into the drawing room and talk with him. He used the room as his study and did his writing there.

"I'll go in the bedroom so I can't hear, if you want me to," Louy said magnanimously.

"*Nien, bitte.* You come," Lotta said quickly. Despite his kindness, Herr Professor could still be intimidating. At Herr Professor's nod, Louy followed them. She curled up on the sofa, her arms hugging her knees, while Lotta sat primly beside her.

"I need to speak with you about your father," Herr Professor said. "I should speak with your mother, but she knows no English."

Lotta's heart leaped, then dropped with an alarming thud. "You haf news of him?"

"No, but I have an idea of how to find him. Louisa tells me he used to work with horses, is that right?"

Lotta nodded.

"For a Baron Something? Can you recall his name?"

"*Nein! Bitte!*" In her alarm, Lotta's English left her. "Excuse, please—Vater said I should never—"

"It's all right, Lotta," Louy soothed.

"Just tell me the sort of work your father did, the sort of work he expected to do here," Herr Professor urged. "We may have made a mistake looking for him only in the city. If he worked with horses . . ."

"It vas in country, *ja!*" Lotta's eyes suddenly lit. "He t'ought . . . he vork vit horses . . . racehorses, show horses, army horses . . . in Virginia. Dat vat his friend say."

"He might have tried to get to Virginia," Louy put in.

Lotta shook her head firmly. "*Nein.* He try already. Too far. Too much money. He haf to stay here till he earn."

"But he may have tried looking for work outside of Boston. He wouldn't know there were no horse farms or racing near. And not speaking English . . . We tried the hospitals and jails— yes, I know, but we must be realistic," Herr Professor said gently, as Lotta flinched. "Suppose something happened, as it did to Karl, and he didn't have the English words to explain? What puzzled me, though, is why he would not have written. Your mother does read German."

Lotta took a deep breath. "He cannot read. Not write, either. He never haf chance to learn. Mutti could teach, but Vater too proud."

"I see," Herr Professor said, looking as though he understood completely. "Well, *I* can write. And I have friends to write to, friends who will help *outside* the city. Be of good cheer, child. We may yet have news of your father before the baby comes."

Lotta worried about leaving Mutti to go to the Alcotts' every day, but Mutti urged her off. "Having a baby is a natural thing! I should know; I've had five, remember? And Mrs. Callaghan will help. You promised Miss Louisa you would help her. If I need you, I'll send Tilda to get you." Mutti laughed. "Anyway, the baby may arrive in the middle of the night. *You* did!"

After that, Lotta took Tilda out and showed her exactly how to walk to the Alcotts' house. She showed Michael, also, just in case.

Three days later Lotta woke shortly after dawn to find Mutti pacing the floor and holding her back. "Shh, don't wake the little ones," Mutti whispered. "Karl's already left for the Market. Make me a cup of tea, will you, Daughter?"

Lotta jumped up. "Is the baby coming?"

Mutti nodded. "But not for hours," she added hastily, as Lotta started for the door. "We won't call Mrs. Callaghan till necessary."

"Are you sure?"

"Liebchen, I *do* know," Mutti said, smiling faintly.

Lotta made tea. She sat on the edge of the mattress to drink hers, and Mutti sipped while walking back and forth. "How long has it been?" Lotta asked.

"About four hours."

"Why didn't you wake me?"

"For what?" Mutti asked. "Don't argue with me, Lottchen. I had enough to handle keeping Karl from noticing. The last thing I wanted was him staying home! When the young ones wake, give them breakfast and send them out to play. Tilda can take them to the Common." Lotta started at that. Mutti never let them go that far without Karl or Lotta with them.

"I don't think so," she said cautiously. "Hansi could be too much of a handful for Tilda." She didn't want to say they might not be safe. "We have the partitions up. They won't notice," she said optimistically. "Or they can play out front, or with the Callaghan children." That would probably be the best idea.

Mutti nodded. "You will stay here, *ja?"*

"Do you think I'd leave?" Lotta asked indignantly.

Wan sunlight began poking through the window. Lena stirred and wakened, followed by the others. Lotta gave them breakfast. "Take Hansi and Lena over to your mattress and keep them there," she said in an undertone to Tilda.

Tilda looked at her. "Is the baby coming?"

Lotta nodded. "When it comes time, I'll tell you where to take the young ones. You'll have to look after them."

"Of course," Tilda said, in much the same tone Lotta had used earlier.

The hours ticked by. Beads of perspiration stood out on Mutti's face now, and occasionally she grimaced and caught her breath. The periods between her labor pains were growing shorter as the contractions themselves grew longer.

"Doesn't take me this long, usually," she muttered to Lotta. "Not after first time." She frowned. Then she staggered slightly and reached out to hold onto the wall.

Lotta ran to her. "Is something wrong?"

"Not wrong. Hard!" Mutti took a deep breath. "I think I lie down for a while."

Lotta helped her. Mutti's face looked so pale it frightened her. "Are you *sure* there's nothing wrong?" she asked.

Mutti didn't answer. Her lips framed the words. "Mrs. Callaghan."

"Get Mrs. Callaghan!" Lotta called over to Tilda. *"Now!"*

Tilda ran out of the room, the door banging behind her. Lena sniffled. The door opened again.

"Mrs. Callaghan?" Lotta called.

"Nah. 'Tis me," Michael's voice answered.

Lotta jumped up and looked around the partition. Michael was standing in the doorway, keeping his eyes away, with Tilda by him. "Ma's off to work," Michael said. "She left at dawn an' won't be back till supper. Is it the bairn?" he asked, as Lotta gasped.

"Ja." Lotta thought swiftly. "Go to Frau Alcott," she said. "Tell her the baby is coming and we need her. And take the young ones with you and leave them there!" Louy wouldn't mind, she knew.

Tilda for once obeyed promptly, pulling on her jacket and

buttoning Lena into hers. Michael was already doing the same for Hansi.

"What's happening?" Mutti asked wearily. Lotta told her quickly, and Mutti nodded.

Michael left, taking the others.

"I think I should walk again," Mutti gasped, and Lotta helped her up. With the children gone, she pushed back the partitioning coverlets and opened the window slightly to let in fresh air. She stacked the mattresses near the window so Mutti could lie down more easily. Then she slid an arm around Mutti's waist and helped her walk.

The clock chimed again. By now Mutti's back was arching and she had to stop walking every few minutes to hold the wall. Suddenly her back arched sharply and she cried out and slumped against Lotta.

"Mutti, what is it?"

Mutti shook her head. "Lie down," she murmured. Lotta steered her to the mattresses and lowered her to them. Perspiration stood out on Mutti's face, and her nightgown clung to her. Her hands gripped Lotta's wrists and then released them.

"Water," she whispered.

Lotta ran for it and held the cup to Mutti's lips. Mutti sipped briefly, then her face twisted again.

"I'm here, Mutti! Hold onto me."

Mutti did so. "You'll be all black and blue before we're finished, Daughter," she joked weakly.

Before we're finished, Daughter. The words included Lotta in Mutti's adult world. Lotta didn't know whether she was more proud or afraid.

Again the clock chimed. Another fifteen minutes. *Where was Frau Alcott?*

Mutti wet her lips, and Lotta leaned close to hear her words. "Daughter, you are too young for this, but I need you . . . the baby does not come right. I need you to tell me if you see the baby's head."

She gave Lotta specific instructions about what to look for. Lotta obeyed, her heart pounding. Suddenly her stomach lurched. She lifted her head, avoiding Mutti's eyes. *"Lieber Gott, what do I do?"* she prayed.

Footsteps pounded up the stairs. The door was flung open. "Frau Alcott—" Lotta cried out gratefully.

"It's me. Marmee's gone for the day," Louy's voice answered. As Lotta swung round to stare at her, Louy ran over quickly.

Michael, standing in the doorway, took one look at Lotta's face and breathed, "Holy Mother an' all the saints," and it wasn't swearing.

"The baby's coming wrong end first," Lotta said baldly.

Louy caught her breath. "What was the name of the doctor who took care of your mother when she had pneumonia?" Lotta supplied it quickly, and Louy swung on Michael. "You heard. He's on Washington Street, near School Street. On the way to the Market. Find him! And send him back here *fast!* Tell him to take a cab! Tell him Mrs. Alcott says he should come, and tell him why! *Mrs.* Alcott, not me, understand?"

Michael nodded and dashed away.

Louy threw off her shawl, rolled up her sleeves, and washed her hands. "Don't worry, I'm a good nurse," she said cheerfully. "Although I can't say I've delivered anything but cats before this. Now, find us both aprons, and bring a washcloth and a bowl of cold water." She knelt down beside Mutti and began stroking back her hair.

Lotta brought aprons and water and knelt down by Louy. Together they got Mutti out of her nightgown and sponged her with cool water. They changed the damp sheet for a dry one and covered her with another. Mutti grasped Lotta's hands in a viselike grip. She closed her eyes, and her lips moved as though she were praying. Then her eyes opened again.

"Daughter."

The words were a bare whisper. Lotta bent so that her ear was close to Mutti's lips.

"If anything happens—take care of children—"

"*Mutti, don't*—"

The hands gripped tighter. "Baptized." Lotta nodded, her throat choking. "Look after Karl—"

Blessedly, the door creaked. Then the doctor was there, lifting Lotta to her feet, saying, "Take this young lady out, Miss Louisa. I'll take over."

Lotta fought against Louy's arms. "*I can't leave Mutti!*"

"Yes, you can!" Louy said sternly. "The doctor needs room to work. You've done everything right, Lotta. Everything you could. The doctor knows what to do. Why, he's probably turned babies right end up hundreds of times!"

Michael was waiting on the landing. "Come inter our place," he said gruffly. "No one home but me an' th' girls. I made some right strong tea." The tea was black as ink, and a spoon would have stood straight up in it. But Lotta was grateful for the thought, and for the comfort of their presence.

From across the landing, despite the closed door, she could hear the muffled sounds Mutti was making as she labored, and presently a faint, outraged cry. Then there was a knock on the Callaghan door and it opened before Michael could reach it. The doctor came in, carrying a bundle. "You have a new brother, Miss Lotta. Safe and sound!"

"Mutti—?"

"She's safe and sound, too, just very tired. This young man gave her quite a time!" Lotta jumped up and streaked toward the doorway. The doctor stopped her. "Hold on, young lady! Aren't you going to take your brother with you?"

He deposited the bundle in Lotta's arms. From inside the towels a tiny fist waved and an indignant dark-eyed face looked back at her. Lotta started to laugh. "Oh, you're another fighter, aren't you? Like me and Karl! *Guten Tag, Johannes!*"

Chapter Eleven

March 1849

Lotta and the young ones spent that night with the Alcotts, after Frau Alcott had arrived at the Mullers, breathless and relieved to find that all was well. "Your daughter and mine took care of me," Mutti told her, and Lotta translated. "Dey are good Fraulein."

"What does that mean?" Louy asked. "I recognize *Frau* for 'woman.' But Fraulein?"

"Is like *Liebchen*, dear little one, instead of *Liebe*. Means 'small women.' Young women, but not children."

"Little women?" Louy asked.

Lotta nodded.

Frau Alcott nodded approvingly. "I like that term. More than girls, though young in age. *Adults*, but young. Much more character to that than 'young ladies.' Goodness knows I've met plenty of ladies, young and old, who aren't mature!"

At any other time, staying overnight at the Alcotts would have been thrilling, but this night Lotta was reluctant, though both mothers insisted. Louy pulled Lotta aside.

"You really must, you know. Your mother needs a peaceful night, and the young ones would feel strange at our place without you." Louy laughed. "You can sleep with me, since Annie's not home, and the little girls can sleep crosswise on the bed with Lizzie and May. We've done that sort of thing before, often. But I'm not sure where to put Karl!"

"He could stay with Michael," Lotta suggested, so that was how it was arranged. Mutti held up weary arms to kiss both Lotta and Louy, and they started off, carrying clothes for the night and leaving Mutti in Frau Alcott's capable hands.

Back on Dedham Street, they found Lizzie cooking supper and May, predictably, putting on airs to impress the Muller young ones. Fortunately, they couldn't understand a word she said and thought she was very funny. Herr Professor looked up from the book he was reading by the stove. "I should like to talk to you after supper, Carlotta. You, too, Louisa." So in the evening they withdrew, as before, into the drawing room. The small fire on the hearth flickered cozily on the books with their gilded bindings, the rich red of the Turkish carpet covering the table.

Herr Professor closed the door after they entered. "Little pitchers," he said cryptically, and Lotta knew he was referring to May. Lotta sat on the sofa and clasped her hands together.

"Is this about *mein Vater?*" she asked directly.

"I need more information. It is very difficult to identify a person who does not speak the language and neither reads nor writes. I forgot to ask you what your father looks like. Is he short or tall?"

Lotta searched for just the right words. "Tall, but not like you. Up to your mouth, maybe. And straight. Military straight." Herr Professor had a pronounced stoop. "Man of the outdoors, *ja?* Much like Karl. But brown hair, brown eyes, brown beard." Louy fetched May's pad and crayons, and Lotta drew a picture of how Vater's hair and beard were cut.

"That description could fit a number of men. Are there any distinguishing marks?" Herr Professor, too, sought for just the

right words. "Anything about how he looks that is part of him
alone? Like a birthmark, or a scar?"

For a minute Lotta didn't breathe. Then she said, carefully,
"Ja, scar. Like this."

She picked up May's pad and drew it with the red crayon,
a jagged line starting at the outer corner of the right eye and
slashing across the face.

She heard Louy draw her breath in sharply. Herr Professor
took the pad and studied it. At last he said gently, "Thank
you, Lotta. This will be every helpful." He rose, indicating the
interview was over.

It was fun sharing a bed with Louy as if she were a sister,
whispering in the dark until very late. The tension of the day
had left Lotta unguarded and very tired, but she couldn't sleep.
She told Louy of the scary moments before Louy had arrived,
and Louy told Lotta about the baby boy who had been born
to the Alcotts when Louy was six. "He only lived a few moments, but I think Marmee still misses him," Louy said. "You're
so lucky, Lotta. Three brothers! I do like boys."

"You can have Karl anytime you want," Lotta said darkly,
and Louy chuckled.

In the morning Lotta went back home, taking the young
ones with her. Karl had already left, but he had seen Mutti
and the baby.

"He is so glad it is another boy!" Mutti chuckled. "He's just
annoyed Johannes does not look like him." The baby was dark-
haired and dark-eyed, like Vater. "If only your father could
see him!"

Lotta didn't answer. The strange conversations with Herr
Professor gave her hope, but she didn't want Mutti to hope
and be disappointed.

It was one of the few times Mutti had referred to Vater since
the first week he'd been gone. That had been almost three
months ago, and to Lotta's relief, she didn't pursue the subject
now. Mutti's mind was on the baby, and on housecleaning. "I

was so ashamed, *Herr Doktor* and Frau Alcott seeing this place so dirty!" Mutti ran her finger over the doorframe and looked with disgust at the greasy soot she had dislodged. "After the fever, I felt too weak to scrub, as I meant to before the baby came! *Now*, we spring clean!"

Mutti made Karl take the mattresses outdoors and beat them, and told him to buy some strong lye soap out of the weekly allowance Gus was giving him. Then she, Lotta, and Tilda scrubbed the room from top to bottom while Lena watched baby Johannes in his basket out on the landing. Even Hansi was pressed into service. "You think your father does not know how to scrub?" she demanded, when Hansi protested that it was women's work. "How do you think he kept the baron's stables so clean? He had stableboys to do that, *ja*, but he worked with them! He did not want animals or family to be near anything not clean!"

"That was different," Hansi insisted, his lip stuck out.

"No, it's not," Karl said, coming home up the stairs and overhearing. "You should hear Gus talk about dirt! Bad for business, bad for people! You think he didn't make me scrub the stall before I came home?" He displayed his reddened, callused hands with a kind of pride.

"I'm surprised he puts up with you," Lotta said slyly, glancing at his stained shirtfront.

"That's all you know, then!" Karl retorted, grinning. "He likes me!"

The Mullers' cleaning went on for a full week, for Mutti insisted everything *in* the room be cleaned as well as the room itself. She even begged the loan of a flatiron from the Alcotts and ironed clothes, bedding, and the curtains Lotta found discarded in a Beacon Hall dustbin and carried home. Mutti's skills as a needlewoman were exquisite, and she saw this as an opportunity to give her three daughters practical lessons. She also informed Michael that it was every man's duty to know how to darn his own stockings, sew on his own buttons, and press his trousers. Since Johannes's birth Michael had appointed himself an honorary uncle, which made him practically a member of the Muller family.

"He has better stuff in him that those brothers of his do," Mutti admitted to Lotta. "It's only our duty to encourage that, *nicht wahr*, Daughter?"

"Oh, yes, Mutti," Lotta said hastily, and tried not to look too pleased.

Even Karl had softened toward Michael lately. He reported to Lotta and Mutti that Michael was now looking for honest work in the Market, too. So on Sunday afternoon, the day after the cleaning was complete, Mutti invited Michael and his mother to come in for tea. When Lotta opened the door at their knock, her jaw dropped. Michael was not only wearing the shirt and knickers that Mutti had helped him mend, he had put on a tie! His scrubbed face shone "as bright as the map o' Ireland," as his mother put it. She, too, was dressed up, in the hat and gown she had worn to midnight church on Christmas Eve, and an embroidered apron. She handed Mutti a basket covered with a napkin. Inside was a crocheted lace cap and jacket for Johannes, and a loaf of fragrant bread.

"Real Irish lace. Me mither taught me to make it when I was a bairn. I'm right sorry I weren't here to help ye when the wee one came, Miz Muller," Mrs. Callaghan said. "An' that there's soda bread."

They were all having tea and bread together when a knock came at the door.

"That may be Louy. I invited her to stop by," Lotta said, and flew to answer it.

Herr Professor stood in the doorway, in a fine broadcloth coat and tall hat. And beside him—

Lotta cried out and, to her everlasting shame, almost fainted.

Vater. He was pale and he was gaunt. He was balancing on a crutch, with his left leg bent and bandaged. There was a new scar on his worn face. But unmistakably and finally, he was

Vater. There was a clink of china and the sound of a chair toppling as Mutti ran to meet him. The children followed.

"Careful! Don't throw the man off balance, he's had a hard enough time already," Herr Professor cautioned, with Lotta trying to translate. In her excitement, almost all of her newly learned English seemed to have vanished. But she made an effort as soon as Vater and Herr Professor were seated.

"Sure an' it's good ye'r back, sir, an' we're right glad ter see ye. Michael, *come!*" Mrs. Callaghan tactfully left, dragging Michael with her. Herr Professor would have gone, also, but Lotta clung to him.

"*Bitte, mein Herr!* You must explain!"

So, talking in English and in German, overlapping each other, the two men told a story as exciting as anything Louy could create. Vater had seen, in a paper lying in the Market, a picture of a farm with horses. He couldn't read the words, but what seemed like a name beneath the picture matched a name he saw on a signboard by the railroad station. Where there were horses, there might be work. Vater had shown picture and word to the ticket-seller in the railroad station, and the official had put him on a railroad car. He had had just enough coins with him to pay for the ticket.

"*Schatz*, how did you expect to get back home?" Mutti asked, smiling through tears. He had meant to earn the passage, of course, Vater replied. But after traveling for quite a while, something had happened. There had been a bull on the tracks. The engineer had braked too sharply, but even so, he had hit the animal, and the car had leapt the tracks.

"You went to help the bull, didn't you?" Mutti said, knowing the answer.

Vater smiled, too. "*Ja*, but once I saw he was all right, I went to help passengers."

After that he didn't know what had happened, not till he woke up to find himself lying bandaged and immobile in a nursing home, with no one able to understand what he tried to say.

Herr Professor took up the story. "At first the train had just gone off the tracks, but it was leaning over a gully, and several passengers had fallen into it from the open cars. Herr Muller went down to help rescue them. He and the engineer got them all out. But then the engine began to fall farther, pinning the engineer. Herr Muller tried to push the engine upright so the engineer could escape. Instead, it fell on both of them. The engineer was killed, and Herr Muller's leg was broken badly in two places. He was unconscious for some time. One of the passengers whose wife Herr Muller had helped saw to it he was taken to the nursing home and paid for his care. But then they left to return to England, without seeing the notice I had put in the Boston paper about Herr Muller being missing. I didn't have a description of him at the time, and apparently no one at the nursing home read the Boston paper. The doctor tried to get Herr Muller to write his name and address but concluded his arm was too bruised for him to manage it."

It took a lot of time for Lotta to translate all this. In the middle of it, Johannes woke up and started exercising his lungs. Lotta ran and brought him to Vater, for Mutti was too busy holding Vater's hands to do so. Vater smiled broadly.

"Johannes?" he asked.

"*Ja*, we were right. Johannes. Three of each we have now." Mutti laughed. "Lena, be careful! You'll spill the baby, and you mustn't try to sit on Vater's lap. You could hurt his leg! *Liebchen*, you look so tired!"

Herr Professor rose. "I must leave you to your reunion."

"*Nein! Bitte!* We still do not know how you found him," Lotta pleaded.

"Why, I circulated the description you gave me among my acquaintances in the countryside. When one response sounded likely, I mailed that friend a drawing my daughter Abbie May had made of you. The likeness was strong enough that your father recognized it at once. My friend notified me, and I went and fetched him home. That is all."

"*All?* How can we thank you properly—" And then Lotta could contain herself no longer. She flew at the tall, stooped figure, stood as tall as she could on tiptoes, and kissed him on the cheek.

"There, there, child. Mrs. Alcott and I are only happy we were able to help. If your father is well enough, will you please bring him to call on me at my home tomorrow afternoon?" Herr Professor bowed himself out, leaving the Mullers to an evening of tears and laughter and much talk.

The meeting the following afternoon was quite different. For one thing, only Herr Alcott was at home. This was, he made courteously clear, a meeting between two gentlemen, and Lotta was there only as translator.

Afterward Lotta was not at all sure how she had managed. It began with an exchange of courtesies and an inquiry into how Vater's leg was doing. Vater complimented Herr Professor on May's drawing ability. Then Herr Professor put it to Vater bluntly.

"It should not have been necessary for a child to be able to draw in order for us to find you. Suppose we had not?"

Vater was taken aback. "I regret that I have not had time yet to learn English, as I intend."

"Excellent. Of course, you will. But what puzzled me was that you did not even try to send a word in German to your wife."

Lotta closed her eyes and prayed hard. Her prayer was answered. Herr Professor did not reveal what she had told him.

"You cannot read or write, can you, Herr Muller?" Herr Professor said quite calmly. "Young men born in America are fortunate. They are almost always able to get a good, free education while still children. I have been to England. I know it is quite different in the Old World. But for goodness' sake, as an intelligent man who is blessed with a wife and children who can read and write, why did you not have your wife teach you? You must have known it would be useful!"

"It is not seemly for a wife to teach her husband," Vater said stiffly. "Or for a grown man to be taking lessons."

"*Seemly*, sir?" Herr Alcott's eyebrows rose. "Was it seemly for her to be forced to worry, to keep home and children functioning for months, with no news of you and a child coming? I may tell you, Herr Muller, that I have a very intelligent wife, and I went into marriage expecting to teach her much. In the nearly nineteen years since, I have learned almost as much from her as she from me. Do you lose respect for me because of that? And do you wish to learn to read and write, or do you not?"

It took some time for Lotta to translate this into German. She used the German-English dictionary, to be absolutely correct, and she did not look at her father as she said the words. Fortunately, after a silence, Vater laughed ruefully.

"*Ja*, I wish to learn to read and write. And *nein*, I do not lose respect. My daughter has told me you are a great man. A professor."

"And I am still learning. Should I be ashamed of that?"

"*Nein!*"

"Excellent." Herr Professor nodded. "Then I, Herr Professor, shall teach you your letters and your numbers, while your leg recovers. I shall teach you English words, and you shall teach me German ones, as our daughters teach each other!" His rare, shy smile flashed. "But you had better have your wife teach you writing. I have been told mine is nothing worth copying! You will allow this?"

Vater pulled himself to his feet, over Lotta's protest, and managed a formal bow. "I should be most grateful."

"Then we understand each other," Herr Professor said, with satisfaction. "I hope you will not be offended," he said, as he walked them to the door, "but I have friends in the West who may know of employment for a man like you. That is, if he is sober, dependable, and learning English, and he can read a little. I understand you are experienced with animals, particularly horses. There is little work of that sort in Boston. But the opportunities in our western territories, like Ohio or Kentucky, are unlimited. Have I your permission to pursue this on your behalf?"

"*Jawohl.*" The two men bowed again and shook hands.

"Oh, yes," he added as he opened the door, "I understand you were in charge of horses for a baron. Is this true? Perhaps he would write you a letter of recommendation."

Lotta froze.

For a minute everything hung in the balance. Then Vater said stiffly, "*Nein. Nicht vondem baron. Auf Wiedersein.*" He began to hobble quickly away.

Lotta ran after him. "Vater, it just slipped out. No name, no place. Nothing I shouldn't say . . . *Liebe Vater,* I'm sorry!"

"Very well, Daughter. We will speak no more of it." But his face looked gray.

He called me "Daughter," Lotta thought. *Not "child."* But her heart was heavy.

That was not the end of it. The next day, as she and Louy were working their way through the German-English dictionary, there was a strain in the air. They were working as they often did. Lotta would turn to a German word and teach Louy pronunciation, and Louy would teach her how to say it in English. Then it would be Louy's turn with an English word. Or they would each look up words in the other's language that they didn't understand. Often, as they did this, they would come upon other words that interested them. Today, Louy's eye fell on the German word "*Schloss.*"

"Does it mean castle?"

"*Nein.* Not so grand. No—" Lotta drew a castle tower in the air.

"Not so old? Not so large? Where a baron might live, but not a grand duke? . . . There *was* a baron, wasn't there, Lotta? Father said your father said no."

Lotta didn't answer.

"I know the difference between plain truth and exaggeration when I hear it," Louy said after a moment. "You *weren't* spinning stories, were you? Lotta, what's wrong? You're shivering."

"*Nichts,*" Lotta whispered. And then she *was* shaking.

Louy hitched her chair close and took Lotta's hands in hers. "I think you'd better tell me," she said. "It's about the trouble, isn't it? And you're afraid. Maybe I can help. I give you my solemn vow I'll tell no one unless you give permission. And I keep my promises."

"I break one if I tell you," Lotta murmured. "But I t'ink I must, or you t'ink vorse of Vater than is truth." She drew a shuddering breath as Louy waited.

"Ven de baron—ven he was alive, he was *gut* to Vater. *Respect* him. Vas my—" She stopped to look up the word *"godfather."* "But his nephew, de next baron, vas cruel man, hate Vater. Vanted us out of house vich old baron's vill said ve could live in . . . one day, one of de horses t'rew him. He seize whip an' try to beat horse to death. Vater rushed in an' grabbed whip away, and Baron drew his sword . . . dat is how Vater got scar. Den baron pull pistol an' turn on horse." She drew another breath. "Vater take de whip an'—stop him. Nobody see. Afterward—baron is lying on ground, all bloody. Vater not know if dead or alive. Only know he must run. Only take time to tell Mutti he change name, meet her in Hamburg. Three nights later, soldiers, *Politzei,* come looking for Vater, but they not find."

"Was the man dead, Lotta?" Louy asked gently.

Lotta shook her head. "No. But not good for Vater to hit baron. Next day ve leave, too. Go to Hamburg, find Vater, take boat to Boston." She turned to Louy imploringly. "You understand? Must not speak of baron! Could send Vater back to Germany, to prison—"

"I don't think so," Louy said thoughtfully. "That's the sort of thing that brought a lot of people to America from the begin-

107

ning. Of *course* he had to stop that man from beating an animal to death! Your father's a hero, Lotta. In the war, in the train accident. Father says so. This is another example of his heroism. Please let me tell my father, Lotta. He'll keep the secret, and maybe he can help."

After a moment, Lotta nodded slowly.

In an incredibly short number of days, or so it seemed to the Mullers, Herr Professor called on them with news that there was a job as livestock manager waiting for Vater in Cincinnati, Ohio. "Tell him there are Germans there," Herr Professor said to Lotta, who was again translating. "The farmer's wife is Swiss, so she speaks German, and her father who lives with them does also. And there are horses."

He went on to explain the terms of the arrangement. Vater must go to Ohio alone now, to prove himself. Frau Alcott would raise the travel money somehow. After six months, if Vater had proved he was a good and sober worker, the employer would pay the cost of bringing the rest of the family out to join him. Herr Professor would himself provide a character reference for Vater and would send the employer a copy of a newspaper story about the railroad accident. Was Vater interested?

Vater was.

Chapter Twelve

April 1849

Almost before the Mullers had time to think, Vater was gone. He was still pale from his hospital confinement, but his family saw a hopeful look in his eyes, one they had not seen for some time. Somehow, Frau Alcott put together a complete "traveling outfit" for him—a decent, though somewhat worn, suit of American clothes; scarcely worn boots; and a hat like the ones other American men wore in the country. Rolled in what looked like a blanket but what the Alcotts called a "traveling rug" were his working smocks and trousers, his boots and heavy stockings for working with animals, and his nightshirts and underclothing, all held securely by a heavy leather strap. All the Mullers and Herr Professor went to the railroad station to see him off. Afterward, Herr Professor went to his meeting room, Karl escorted Mutti and the younger children home before going to the Market, and Lotta went to Louy.

"Cheer up!" Louy said instantly, when she saw Lotta's face. "Think how splendid this will be for your father! Think how hard he'll be working so he can send for you *soon.*"

Lotta wiped her eyes, her accent returning under the stress of her emotion. "Ve jus' get him back, ve lose again. Is so hard—"

Louy hugged her. "I know. Believe me, I know. But you have to be strong, Lottchen. For the young ones, and your mother." She pressed a handkerchief into Lotta's hand. "Now, wipe your eyes, and blow, and let's talk about something pleasant. Have you forgotten, Fraulein Muller, that another important event looms ever closer?" When Lotta looked at her blankly, she laughed. "Your birthday, silly! Have you forgotten that Annie and I promised you a celebration?"

"Has been years since such," Lotta confessed.

"Well, this one will make up for that, I guarantee! Have an apple, and let's plan! What was special about the birthday celebrations you remember?"

Lotta gazed off into space, and out of nowhere came the memory of cloves and cinnamon. The memory was so sharp, so sudden, she could almost smell them.

"What is it?" Louy asked gently.

"Scripture cake."

"Tell me," Louy said, watching her closely.

Lotta felt for words. "The—how you call it, instruction?—come down in Mutti's family. Spice cake. Everything you put in, you read the Scripture first that tells about it. Always ve haf—have—for Easter and my birthday."

"Will your mother remember how to make it?" Louy asked.

Lotta nodded. "Ach, ja. Mutti know—knows—by heart the verses to read. Also, I t'ink is written in Grosspapa's Bible."

"Then that's what we'll have," Louy said with decision. "Scripture cake. We'll get the ingredients. Maybe Karl can get some from that Gus at the Market. Your mother can make it here, in our oven."

Lotta shook her head. "Here, yes, is fine. But all make together. Is part of—" She searched for the word.

"Ritual?" Louy supplied. "Then that's what we'll do. I know Marmee will like it, and that way we can learn to make it, too. As for the rest of the celebration, we'll have that Alcott style!"

And not a word would she offer as to what that meant.

Lotta's birthday dawned beautiful with spring sunshine. After Johannes had been nursed and bathed and the room set straight, Mutti, Lotta, Tilda, Hansi, Lena, and the baby set off for Dedham Street. Karl ran down to the Market for the produce Gus had promised him. He was back so fast that he reached the Alcotts' door before it had been opened for the Mullers, and he had Michael with him. "Met me in the Market, an' I said I'd help," Michael said.

Louy liked Michael. He was, she murmured to Lotta, a boy after her own heart. And she was impressed with Karl's behavior. "Looks like everything he's been through has been good for him," she whispered.

Karl and Michael added their bundles to the foodstuffs the Alcotts had already set forth on the kitchen table along with spoons, knives, cups, plates, a pitcher of milk, a bowl of eggs, and a huge blue mixing bowl. The Alcotts were already wrapped in aprons, and Mutti produced aprons for her girls. Louy tied huge towels around Michael, Karl, and Hansi.

Such a chopping and grating, a peeling and measuring was there then! At last Mutti said, smiling, "All is ready. Come!" She said it in German, but its meaning was clear.

They all gathered around the table. Mutti held Grosspapa Lindmeier's Bible, and Frau Alcott held *her* father's Bible. Mutti read the first verse of the instructions aloud, and then Frau Alcott repeated it in English.

"Judges 5:25. *He asked water, and she gave him milk; she brought forth butter in a lordly dish.*"

Everyone laughed when Frau Alcott translated that, for the butter was sitting on an old cracked plate. Mutti turned it into the big mixing bowl and beat it with a wooden spoon till it was light.

Now it was Annie's turn. She took her Grandfather May's Bible from her mother.

"Jeremiah 6:20. *To what purpose cometh there to me incense from Sheba, and the sweet cane from a far country?*" Mutti read the verse in German as Annie poured molasses onto the butter and beat it in.

Then came Louy. "First Kings 4:22. *And Solomon's provision for one day was thirty measures of fine flour, and threescore measures of meal.*" She poured in brown flour and white, mixing after each addition until the mixture was stiff.

Karl was next. Mutti looked at him sternly and handed him Grosspapa's Bible. He squinted at it ferociously, but made it through. "Amos 4:5. *And offer a sacrifice of thanksgiving with leaven, and proclaim and publish the free offerings; for this liketh you, O ye children of Israel, saith the Lord God.*" He took a deep breath and reached for the soda as Mutti rescued the precious Bible quickly. In went the baking soda, cinnamon, and cloves.

"Michael is next, I believe," Frau Alcott passed her Bible to him. He stared at it as if it burnt his fingers. Louy saved him from embarrassment.

"I'll read it for him, so he won't have to do penance for reading a Protestant Bible," she announced. *She's guessed he can't read,* Lotta thought, and flashed Louy a grateful smile. Louy winked back, but her voice as she read was properly sober. "Genesis 43:11. *Carry down the man a present, a little balm, and a little honey, spices, and myrrh, nuts, and almonds.*" She looked at Michael, and he sprinkled in a pinch of ground ginger.

It was Lizzie's turn now. "Jeremiah 17:11," she read. *"As the partridge sitteth on eggs, and hatcheth them not: so he that getteth riches, and not by right, shall leave them in the midst of his days, and at his end shall be a fool."* Into the stiff dough she stirred the beaten eggs.

"Sure, an' did ye really find partridge's eggs in th' city?" Michael marveled in a whisper. Lotta frowned at him, and Lena giggled.

Mutti passed Grosspapa Lindmeier's Bible to Lotta. "Judges 4:19. *And he said unto her, Give me, I pray thee, a little water to drink: and she opened a bottle of milk, and gave him drink.*" Lotta passed the Bible back to Mutti and was reaching for the pitcher when Frau Alcott interrupted.

"Lotta can read the English version herself," she said, and handed it to Lotta. Louy smiled encouragingly. Lotta read it carefully, watching her *v*'s and *th*'s. She returned the Bible and stirred the buttermilk into the bowl. It was now growing very full.

"It's going to overflow," Lena whispered. Mutti shushed her.

Tilda read her verse proudly, stumbling only once. "First Samuel 14:25. *And all they of the land came to a wood, and there was honey upon the ground.*" She spooned in the fragrant honey. By now the contents of the bowl smelled heavenly.

May's turn. "First Samuel 30:12. *And they gave him a piece of cake of figs, and two clusters of raisins; and when he had eaten, his spirit came again to him,*" she read dramatically. In went the raisins. She reached for the figs, but Frau Alcott, who had looked ahead at the next verse, stopped her.

Lotta guided Hansi through his reading. "Nahum 3:12. *All thy strongholds shall be like fig trees with the first ripe figs; if they be shaken, they shall fall even into the mouth of the eater.*"

"I wish they would," Karl whispered, in German whose meaning was all too clear, as Hansi proudly added the figs. It was nearly lunchtime, and Karl was restless. Mutti took the spoon from Hansi and handed it to Karl.

"Stir!" she ordered. Everyone chuckled when Karl had trouble working the figs into the thick cake batter without its overflowing. Karl reddened, but then he laughed, too.

It was Lena's turn now, but she was too young for the reading. "May I?" Herr Professor asked Mutti with a courtly bow. When she nodded, his voice rang out. "Numbers 17:8. *And it came to pass that on the morrow, Moses went into the tabernacle of witness; and behold, the rod of Aaron for the house of Levi was budded, and brought forth buds, and bloomed blossoms, and yielded almonds.*"

He lifted Lena so she could tip in the almonds and helped her stir. Then he set her down and, without needing to look at the Bible, quoted, "Song of Solomon 2:5. *Stay me with flagons, comfort me with apples.*"

Lotta fought back a smile. There were no apples in Mutti's recipe, but by now the Mullers knew Herr Professor was wild for apples. They were being added just to please him.

The recipe was complete. Mutti and Frau Alcott poured the batter into two pans and fussed with the temperature of the oven. Annie and Lizzie began the washing-up. Louy turned on the others firmly. "All right, everyone! Out! You, too, Lotta! Everyone goes except Frau Muller and the baby, if she wants to stay! Not you, May! I need you here!"

Mutti decided to stay. Karl had to go back to the Market, but Michael proposed taking the young Mullers to the Common. They went, accompanied by a basket of pretzels and apples the Alcotts pressed on them. "Come back at four! Not a minute before or after!" Louy warned.

Time passed slowly, for Lotta's brain was racing with curiosity and Mutti had ordered them not to do anything that would get them dirty. "As if I would," Lotta thought, smoothing the skirts of Annie's altered dress. Mutti had mended Grossmama Lindmeier's apron and had promised Lotta could wear it for the party.

At last the clock near the Common stood at a quarter to four. Karl and Lotta were supervising a general handwashing and face-wiping at the fountain. Karl and Michael slicked their hair down with their hands. Lotta dried the younger children's hands on her petticoat, for want of anything better. They hurried back to Dedham Street.

The Alcotts' door was locked.

Lotta, frowning, lifted the knocker and used it vigorously.

The door was opened by May, wearing one of Lizzie's white dresses looped up with strange and wonderful ribbons, and faded cloth roses in her curls.

"Enter, O Princess of the Day!" she chanted, sweeping a grand curtsy that almost rocked her off her feet. Karl and Michael choked and poked each other in the ribs. Led by Lotta, they all went inside.

There was Mutti in Frau Alcott's armchair, changed into her best dress and wearing the pretty lace cap she reserved for great occasions. Frau Alcott was also wearing a lace cap, and Herr Professor had a stickpin in his fine cravat.

"May I escort you, Miss Muller?" he asked, bowing and offering her his arm.

Lotta drew herself up tall and tucked her arm through his. He conducted her to a throne that was his writing chair draped with a piece of old brocade, with one of the Alcotts' sofa cushions as a footstool. Frau Alcott nodded the other children to places on the floor. The mantel was garlanded with greens and blossoms, and more green garlands framed the wide drawing-room doorway, now hung with faded, still elegant brocade curtains. Somewhere behind them a gong sounded.

Louy appeared, dressed like a man in high yellow boots, doublet, hose, and a grand plumed hat. Her hair was pinned up, and she wore a sooty mustache. Sweeping off her hat, she bowed grandly to Lotta, then to the rest of the audience.

"O Princess Carlotta, we beg to set before you *The Witch's Curse*, an operatic tragedy by Miss Louisa May Alcott, starring the Misses Anna Bronson Alcott, Elizabeth Sewall Alcott, Abigail May Alcott, and the author herself. Let the revels now begin!"

She swept another grand bow and disappeared. The gong sounded again, and the curtains opened jerkily. A gloomy wood appeared, with a cave made of sheets draped over furniture, and a black iron soup pot as a cauldron. A red glow came from within it. Louy stalked in, now wearing a full beard, a slouch hat, and a cloak she twirled grandly. She sang a deep-voiced aria with much sword-slashing.

Then an old hag appeared with a hooked nose and stringy gray hair trailing down over her red and black robe. She cackled and slobbered.

Lena took one look and hid her face in Lotta's skirt. "Shh, it's only Fraulein Alcott," Lotta whispered reassuringly.

The scenes rolled on, with the Alcott sisters playing all the parts. May was funny; she was too careful of her appearance and her clothes to throw herself around dramatically, as her sisters did. Louy had been right, Annie was a good actress. And Louy, Lotta thought, awestruck, was a great writer.

The play built to an operatic finale in which hero and heroine were reunited and left the stage entwined, to be replaced by villain and villainess—also Louy and Annie—staggering on in diabolical death throes. At last they collapsed dramatically upon the stage, having killed each other.

A round of applause, then silence. Then nothing. The corpses lay there, motionless, through a spattering of more applause. Louy's nose began to twitch, and then she gave an enormous sneeze. Titters swept through the audience.

"May! *Close the curtains!*" Louy's voice hissed. The curtains began to jerk, then caught on a corner of the castle wall. Everything—curtains, castle, and haunted wood—collapsed.

Karl, Michael, and Hansi couldn't stop laughing. If Lotta hadn't been enthroned, she would have kicked them. Fortunately, Louy couldn't keep from laughing, either. She jumped up and held out her hands to her sisters, and they all took a bow.

"Now, bundle those props and curtains out of the way, do, so we can go on with the celebration," Frau Alcott ordered, her lips twitching. Michael and Karl, trying to make up for their loud laughter, jumped to help. The "stage effects" vanished as if by magic, leaving a view of the drawing room, also garlanded, with a cloth-covered table in its center. A pile of wrapped gifts waited at one end, and the party feast—or "collation," as May called it—covered the rest.

With bell, gong, flute, and drum, the Alcotts led Lotta to the table, followed by Karl and Michael, carrying the throne. The rest of the guests fell in behind them. Louy crowned Lotta with a laurel wreath. "It's an Alcott tradition," Lizzie whispered when Lotta was feeling overwhelmed.

After the unwrapping of the gifts—a poem by "L. M. Alcott," a crayon drawing by May, a pincushion from Lizzie, a black sateen apron from Annie, and a picture-card with a kind note from Frau Alcott and Herr Professor—came the collation. The Muller tradition of Scripture cake was an enormous success. So were the graham cookies, baked apple slices, cheese, brown bread, and spiced cider provided by the Alcotts. At last, when all had been sated with pleasure and comforted with apples, it was time for the Mullers to leave. Frau Alcott wrapped the second Scripture cake for Lotta to take with her. "I've even put in a birthday candle," she said, smiling. "Keep that for next year. You must put a slice of cake under your pillow tonight and dream good dreams."

The Mullers were full enough of the collation, and weary enough from the day's excitement, to go to bed early, even Mutti. (She generally did now, as she had to wake every few hours to nurse Johannes.) So was Lotta. She tucked her gifts into the trunk for safekeeping and crawled onto the mattress with her sisters, leaving Mutti her mattress to herself. She fell asleep almost at once, and woke again to find the room dark and the clock chiming midnight. No one else was stirring. She lay in bed, being careful not to wake Mutti, thinking about the birthday celebration. If only Vater had been there, it would have been perfect. The play, the presents, the Scripture cake . . .

Lotta sat bolt upright. *I forgot to put a piece beneath my pillow and make a wish,* she thought. She crawled off the mattress and groped for the package cautiously. Her fingers encountered the block of cake, the hard rounded length that was the candle.

It couldn't wake Mutti if she lit the candle over in the corner. She was wide awake, and she really should write the celebration up in her journal, so she'd remember every detail to tell Vater.

It couldn't hurt if she ate another piece of Scripture cake.

Crouched in the far corner near the door, Lotta lit the candle and stuck it to the floor with a bit of melted wax. She cut two slices of cake, wrapped the rest, and bent over her journal. By the time she finished eating one slice of cake and writing, she was very sleepy. She blew out the candle and crawled back to the mattress, tucking the other cake slice and the journal in her pillow sham. Tilda and Lena might think of looking beneath her pillow for the cake, but not inside the sham.

She fell asleep quickly and dreamed about Louy's play. The witch, no longer even slightly like Annie, loomed ten feet tall. The cauldron sent forth leaping flames and an evil smell. The witch was grabbing her, shaking her . . .

"Lotta! *Lotta!*"

She struggled up from sleep.

It was *Karl's* voice shouting. *Karl's* hands were shaking her violently. "Lotta, wake up! *Fire!*"

Chapter Thirteen

April 1849

Lotta sat bolt upright.

The acrid smell was still in the air, and a glow from beyond the rain-spattered window silhouetted Karl kneeling beside her, his eyes glittering with remembered horror. *"The house is on fire!"* he shouted hoarsely.

For an instant she thought he, too, was having a nightmare. The memory of late last night flooded over her—herself, lighting Louy's candle, and writing. Growing sleepy. Crawling into bed.

I know I blew the candle out. I know it! she thought frantically.

Could blowing it have scattered sparks? If so, why weren't there flames right in the room? She struggled to think straight, but she couldn't think of anything except guilt, and fear. And an old nightmare that had been too horribly real.

Everything seemed to happen very slowly, as in a dream. Tilda and Lena, wakened by Karl's voice, were struggling up, rubbing their eyes. Karl was running to the door, reaching for the handle. Fingers of smoke were curling in around the window frame and beneath the door—

Lotta, suddenly wide awake, shouted, *"Don't!"*

It was too late. Karl's hand was already turning the handle. He opened the door only a crack, then slammed it shut. But in that instant, smoke had eddied in. Lotta's throat constricted. That meant the stairway was blocked—

Karl whirled around, pointing at the window. *But we're on the third floor,* Lotta thought in terror.

There was no time to think about that. Lights were flickering outside, and there were sounds of shouting, of gongs clanging. The trancelike spell in the room was broken. Tilda was shaking violently, and Lena was crying. Lotta wrapped them in bedding.

"Crawl to the window, *quickly!*" she ordered. Vater had said once that smoke was least dangerous near the ground. They obeyed, and Karl literally tossed Hansi to them. Then he was waking Mutti.

The baby was crying. Lotta covered her nose and mouth with her pillow and crawled to Johannes's basket. She scooped him swiftly into the pillow and clutched him to her.

The smoke in the room was growing thicker.

"The trunk! Must take!" Mutti shouted to Karl.

"Nein, Mutti—"

"Take!" Mutti panted, crawling toward the window, her pillow against her face.

Karl lifted the trunk and threw it at the window. It went through with a mighty crash, carrying out all the glass. A gust of damp, smoke-laden air eddied in. From below a man's voice was shouting in English. Lotta peered out.

The yard was filled with people. It was lit with a red glow coming from above, but like a miracle, no flames were billowing from the building as Lotta glanced down. *It's a miracle,* she thought giddily. Then the reality sank in. The flames were in the attic . . . in the roof—

The attic, barely high enough to stand in, was directly over the Mullers' heads.

Through her terror, the man's voice penetrated. *"Jump!"*

Lotta stared downward. Directly below the window, on

ground level, a lean-to shed jutted out from the back of the building. It covered the steps that led down to the cellar. Mr. Callaghan and his oldest son, Patrick, were standing on the shed's sloping roof. They had sheets twisted into ropes in their hands, and the trunk beside them. As Lotta watched, Patrick Callaghan pitched the trunk off the roof edge. Mr. Callaghan was motioning fiercely.

"They want us to jump to the shed roof. They'll get us down from there," Lotta gasped, coughing. By now the yard was filled with people, running around or standing in a circle, staring upward. People came pouring through the back doors of the houses fronting on the street behind, bringing buckets, blankets, mattresses. A pile of mattresses already lay on the ground beside the shed. Old Peg-Leg Jackson and two men from the first floor were filling buckets at the backyard pump. But there was no way to get water up to the attic from which, to Lotta's horror, an ominous crackling sound was coming.

"Baby?" Mutti demanded, from behind Lotta's shoulder.

"Here."

Mutti was knotting the Muller bedsheets together. Karl tied one end to the legs of the stove. Mutti tied the other end around Lotta, binding the baby against Lotta as she did so.

"You first," Mutti ordered. "Karl next. I come last."

There was no time to argue. Lotta, with Johannes clutched tightly in the pillow, jumped. Mr. Callaghan and Patrick broke her fall as she reached the shed roof, untied the sheet-rope, and lowered her onto the pile of mattresses below.

Lotta lay there for a moment, breathless, still clutching Johannes and the pillow to her. Then she was being dragged off the mattress so the others could follow. Michael and Mrs. Callaghan came running over.

"Saints alive! Ye've got th' bairn!" Mrs. Callaghan exclaimed, gathering them both in. Incredibly, Johannes had slept through it all.

"Mutti!" Lotta called frantically, as she surrendered the baby to Mrs. Callaghan's motherly arms.

"Hush, she's comin'," Mrs. Callaghan soothed.

She doesn't sound positive, Lotta thought desperately, staring back toward the house. Despite falling rain, the roof was engulfed in flames that spread to the roofs of the houses attached on either side. Karl stood on the shed roof, holding Hansi. As Lotta watched, Patrick Callaghan wrenched him from Karl's arms and tossed him over the edge. Hansi landed on the mattress pile, and Michael ran to lead him off and comfort him. Lotta tried to follow, but Mrs. Callaghan held her back.

"Michael will take care o' him, he will."

Lotta nodded, barely hearing, her eyes fixed on the shed roof, since the upper stories were now swallowed up in smoke. Two smaller figures came down the sheet-rope—Lena, then Tilda. Each in turn was lowered to the ground. Then the shed roof was no longer visible at all. Lotta couldn't breathe. Mrs. Callaghan still held her tightly, but somewhere near them Lena was crying and Tilda, shaking violently, was trying to comfort her. An old woman from the house behind wrapped them in a blanket. Then Karl was nearby, with Hansi telling him how exciting it all was. Lotta shut her eyes tightly and prayed as she had never prayed before.

Then Mrs. Callaghan, an unlikely angel, was murmuring, "Sure, an' here's yer mither now right as rain."

Mutti was lying on the mattress, drawing deep, shuddering breaths. Two men helped her up, and an Italian woman from down the street wrapped her in a shawl. Lotta ran to her, and they clung together.

"The young ones?" Mutti demanded.

"We're all safe. Mrs. Callaghan has the baby." Lotta started to laugh. "Even the trunk is safe!" She laughed until her laughs turned to sobs.

Distantly there was a clanging of bells, and a fire wagon

dashed up, the horses' nostrils flaring. The fire men herded everyone ruthlessly to the next street.

"Move! *Now!* The walls might collapse!" They tried to make Karl leave the trunk, but Karl was too swift for them. He hoisted it in the air above his head and ran with it into the street. The other Mullers followed, and Michael joined them.

"Your family?" Mutti asked him in German. Michael sensed her meaning and pointed to show that they were safe. "How did it happen?" Mutti asked. But this he couldn't understand, and Lotta wasn't up to the effort of translating. They sat on the trunk, or on the muddy ground, in their nightclothes, as the rest of their possessions went up in flames. The vein in Karl's temple was throbbing the way Vater's sometimes did. Mutti looked as though she'd aged in hours. In her arms the baby slept on Lotta's pillow. Tilda was silent, pressing up close by Lotta. Only the two youngest seemed oblivious to danger. The leaping flames were beautiful against the night sky.

Lotta sat like stone, her ears straining. The firemen were working the pump now, pointing their hoses at the building, aided by men and boys from the neighborhood. The fact that she understood some, but not all, of their English was both a blessing and a curse. "Anyone left inside?" she heard, and the careless answer, "Who can know for sure? You know how these immigrants live, packed in like rabbits. Who knows who lives where?"

"That old Mick on the shed says everyone's accounted for 'cept a pair of laborers that lived in the attic," another male voice said. "They could be fried by now, or they could be out somewhere, drinking. Anyway, fire's almost out. Thank God for the rain, or that whole strip of shanties would be gone."

Then the first man again, laughing coarsely. "Too bad it's not. City's getting ruined by all these people. Any idea how th' fire started?" And the careless answer, "You know these Irish. Score to settle. Or smoking in bed. Or someone drunk, over-turning a lamp or a candle . . ."

Lotta froze. "The fire started in the attic, not in our room." She repeated it over and over to herself, as Mrs. Callaghan repeated her rosary prayers.

The rain was falling harder now. Firemen were trying to make people leave, go home, go anywhere. Mutti just sat there dazed as Karl tried to get her to move. "There is nowhere left to go," she whispered.

"We'll go to Frau Alcott, of course," Karl said huskily.

Of course. Lotta rose stiffly, pulling Tilda with her. She gathered in Hansi and Lena and, still clutching her pillow, went to touch Mutti's shoulder. "Karl is right. We go to the Alcotts'."

They walked off through the dark. Somehow, Michael was with them. He and Karl carried the trunk between them.

Dedham Street was all in blackness, for rain clouds veiled the moon. It was Karl, not Lotta, who beat a tattoo on the Alcotts' door. Herr Professor himself came to open it, an old overcoat over his nightshirt. He peered out, then threw the door wide. "Abba!" he shouted, and Frau Alcott, in nightgown and shawl, came running. Then the girls were there, too, exclaiming in shock, drawing them all inside. Louy stoked the fire and Lizzie put the kettle on. They brought blankets; they brought dry clothes. Somehow, under Frau Alcott's deft direction, the refugees were soon dry and warm without and within.

"Of course you were right to come here!" Frau Alcott exclaimed over Mutti's apologies. "Where else? We'll worry about finding a place for you to live tomorrow. Your family, too," she added, with a look at Michael. "For now, what you all need is rest." Tilda was sent to bed with Lizzie and May, while Mutti, Lotta, and Lena had Louy's bed. Johannes slept on Lotta's pillow on the floor by Mutti. Karl, Michael, and Hansi were put on blankets on the kitchen floor, close by the banked fire. Louy would sleep on the drawing-room sofa.

At last they were all settled in place, but Lotta could not sleep. The memory of the candle burned in her brain.

At last she drifted off into a troubled sleep, and woke to the smell of apples.

"Come on, get up!" Tilda called. "Frau Alcott's making *Pfankuchen mit Apfel!*"

Frau Alcott also produced the remains of the Alcotts' loaf of Scripture cake. "This will be as good for breakfast as for dessert," she announced. Lotta thought it would choke in her throat.

"Why aren't you eating?" Mutti asked anxiously. Lotta just shook her head.

"Let the girl be," Louy advised. But she, too, watched Lotta closely.

After breakfast, talk of where to relocate the Mullers and the Callaghans began. Michael volunteered that their priest might be able to find a place for them. "Maybe Gus would let me sleep at the stall," Karl volunteered. "He's said he wished he had a night watchman. Animals come around trying to break in for food. Cats and things," Mutti looked unsure, but Herr Professor spoke up approvingly.

"That is good thinking on your part, young man. Your father would be proud of you. I shall write and tell him how you looked out for your family last night." Karl didn't say anything, but his eyes glowed.

Herr Professor and Frau Alcott conferred about the others. "The one place I can be sure of is the Robinsons'," Frau Alcott said. "They can make space, and will appreciate the need." She turned to Mutti and had Lotta translate. "They are free black friends of ours, very kind, and they understand what it is like to need friends. I'm sure they'll make you welcome."

"Schwartzer?" Mutti asked, puzzled. *"Frei?"* Frau Alcott explained how most people of African descent in America were slaves or escaped slaves, but that the Robinsons were free and had been part of the Boston community for some time. She would write to the Robinsons at once if Mutti permitted, Frau

Alcott said, and ask if they would take all the Mullers except Karl in until Frau Alcott could find them a permanent home.

Mutti nodded. "That will be very kind."

"Lotta will stay here," Louy said decidedly. "I have a great new story bounding round in my head, and she can do my work so I have time to write."

"If Lotta doesn't mind, and so long as my Louy doesn't neglect the sewing she has promised to complete before summer," Frau Alcott said, smiling.

"*Ja, bitte,*" Lotta said in a small voice, and after a moment Mutti agreed.

Michael went off to find his own family, as he was sure he could. Herr Professor went to the Market with Karl to speak with Gus. Frau Alcott wrote a note for Louy to deliver to the Robinsons, and when Louy returned with their response, they all walked Mutti and the children to the Robinsons' home. It was about half an hour's distance from the Alcotts', in a pleasant street blossoming with April flowers. Then Frau Alcott went off about her errands, and Lotta and Louy walked back to Dedham Street. Louy took Lotta into the drawing room and shut the door.

"All right. Tell me," she said.

Lotta looked at her blankly.

"What you're so frightened about. I know the signs."

Lotta swallowed. "The firemen were talking . . . about how the fire started . . ." She repeated the words about the Irish, breaking off to say, "Mutti is right. Never again shall we listen to bad things said about the Irish. Last night they saved our lives. And Mrs. Callaghan and Michael are so kind."

"Good for you!" Lotta said approvingly. "Father always says we must look for the good in everyone, although I'm not sure I could stretch myself to include all of Michael's brothers. I'm glad Michael's not like them. Father's heard bad things about them. Maybe someone did have a score to settle against them, or they were drunk and knocked over a lamp, or something."

Lotta shook her head. *"Nein.* Not lamp. Not them."

Louy looked at her closely, frowning. "What do you mean, *Liebchen?* Tell me."

"I lit a candle. Last night. To write in journal. I blew out before going back to bed." Lotta shrugged, her chin beginning to tremble. "Maybe it not go out entirely."

"Oh, Lotta." Louy gathered her in her arms and hugged her. "It couldn't have been that. Use your head. You all said there were no flames in your room when you awoke. And the firemen said the flames started in the attic. That couldn't have happened from a candle in *your* room. Talk to Father about it," she urged, when Lotta looked dubious. "He'll probably be able to find out for you what *did* happen. Now, think about something pleasant, quick! So you've been writing in your journal, have you?"

Lotta nodded. "Every day. Except, now all gone." Then she jumped. "No! I put journal in pillow sham, with piece of cake. And I bring pillow here!" She ran into Louy's room, returned with the smoke-stained pillow, and unbuttoned it quickly. There was the slice of cake, considerably crumbled. There was the journal.

"The cake might have kept better if you'd wrapped it," Louy said dryly. "Some of the crumbs must have gotten in the journal. The cover's not lying flat." Lotta picked it up, frowning. Her pencil and the candle rolled out.

"Next time, you'll believe me when I tell you something," Louy crowed. "You *didn't* start the fire!"

But I could have, Lotta thought. *I'll never be so careless again.*

The next few days passed quietly, for the Mullers were all exhausted. Lotta paid visits to the Robinsons', and so did Karl, who was staying at the stall, as he'd suggested. She kept up with her English studies and wrote in her journal. She listened to Louy think out loud about the book she intended to write. It was called *The Inheritance* and was very thrilling, though Lotta doubted if Mutti would approve of the subject matter. Louy admitted she didn't think Marmee would, either. "But sensational stories are what publishers want these days, and I mean to make a lot of money through writing as soon as I can!"

"So do I, but I don't know vat at," Lotta admitted.

"You could do fine sewing. The baby clothes you made for Johannes are beautiful, and Marmee's impressed by the sewing you've done to help me out. You have quite a seamstress's skill." Louy had an order from a relative for a set of sheets in fine linen, with monogrammed hems, and sewing on them was getting in the way of her story writing.

"I can help," Lotta offered. "For free."

"No. If you help, you get paid. Anyway, Marmee says I must do the work myself because I promised to. They have to be completed before we go away for the summer." Louy explained that the Alcotts moved regularly, depending on rents and what housing was available, and that friends or relatives of her parents often lent them their fine houses while they themselves were at the seashore for the summer months.

"I hope Frau Alcott can find us a place soon. Cheap," Lotta said. "And clean."

Louy grinned knowingly. "The two don't always go together, don't I know! Cheer up! Your father will be sending for you in six months, I'm sure. And you can always come stay with me, Lotta. Anytime you want."

Everything went well for a week or more. Then, unexpectedly, Gus appeared at the Alcott door at dinnertime and asked to speak to Herr Professor. They were in the drawing room for quite a while, and after Herr Professor saw Gus out, he turned to Lotta, looking sober. "Will you please come inside, child? I need to speak to you about the fire."

Lotta's heart began thumping. "Louy, too, *bitte*," she said. "*Und* Frau Alcott."

"We'll go in the bedroom," Lizzie said discreetly. "Come along, May."

They disappeared, but Herr Alcott led the others into the drawing room anyway. This was clearly a serious matter. When the women were seated, Herr Alcott turned to Lotta directly. "There is no easy way to put this. The fire *was* set. Because of the trouble he was in before, the police are blaming Karl. I'm afraid one of the Callaghan boys, not Michael, suggested that. Apparently there's been bad blood between them."

"*Nein!* Karl *couldn't!*" Lotta jumped up, her hands balled into fists. "Please, you must help him!"

"Are you absolutely sure, child? He has a hot temper. Can you really be sure what he would or wouldn't do? If he comes forward and explains, things will be easier for him—"

"*Nein! You* do not understand! Not fire! Anything but fire, maybe. But not fire!" Lotta took a deep breath. "Ven the *Politzei* come for Vater and find him gone, they go away. But that night they—somebody—torch our house. It haf—vat you call, straw roof—ve almost burned alive. More bad dan here. Karl, Mutti, I vork hard, trying to put out, but could not. Everyt'ing go . . . everything except trunk, same as here. Karl burned on hands and arms, trying. Dat vy Karl so afraid of fire now, more even dan us—" She shook her head firmly, the tears starting. "He vould *not* start fire! My little dog Gretel, she die in fire, Karl burned going back in to try to save—"

There was a long silence. "Then Karl was even more brave the other night than we realized," Herr Professor said quietly. "Gus did not believe Karl could have been involved, and I am glad I can now agree with him."

Frau Alcott put her arms around Lotta. "Do not worry, my dear. My husband will put everything to rights!"

"He can tell the police to start looking into those *bad* Callaghans!" Louy said, her eyes shooting sparks. "Just don't let them start suspecting Michael now, Father. I like that boy!"

"Don't worry," Herr Alcott said. "I quite agree."

Nothing more was said about the matter, except that the Alcotts invited Karl to come to dinner the next evening. And on Sunday afternoon, to Lotta's surprise, Mutti and Karl both arrived at the Alcotts', bringing Johannes. After tea and the remainder of the Scripture cake, Lizzie and May withdrew as if by prearrangement. Herr Professor cleared his throat and turned to Karl. "Your sister will translate for you and your mother what I have to say. This concerns your mother also, but with her permission, I will address myself to you. You have earned that right."

Lotta, startled, looked at her mother as she translated, but Mutti just smiled.

"Your Mr. Gus at the Market thinks very highly of you, Karl. You may not know it, but he told the police very firmly that you could have had nothing to do with the recent fire, and that he had misjudged you in the earlier incident. He says you are becoming a fine man. He came to me because your father was not here. He has a business proposal, but first I would like to hear what you yourself want for your future. To work with animals, as your father does? To go with your family to Cincinnati?"

Karl hesitated, then shook his head. "I like the city. I would like to work here and earn good money. I've learned a lot from Gus."

"The money will come in time," Herr Professor assured him. "For now, Gus would like you to become his apprentice in his Market business." Lotta had to turn to the German-English dictionary for this, but when Mutti understood she looked surprised and rather pleased. So did Karl.

"Do you understand what this would mean?" Herr Professor went on. "It means you enter into a legal contract with Gus. Your father would have to sign for you, or make his mark, since you are not of age. The contract would state that until you are twenty-one, you bind yourself to work for Gus under his direction. He will teach you the business. You will do whatever he requires. You will live in his home and receive all your meals and a suit of clothes every year. Usually apprentices are not paid, but because of your mother's need, Gus is willing to give you a bit of money, not much, every week. When you are twenty-one, you will receive a *fine* suit of clothes, and a sum of money, and a good salary, if you wish to keep on working for Gus. Are you interested in this?"

Karl's answer needed no translating. *"Jawohl!"*

"You had better discuss it with your mother," Herr Professor said, with a little smile. "Then, if you both agree, I will send the legal papers to your father. Someone in Cincinnati will translate them for him."

Within the week, the apprenticeship contract was back from Cincinnati, signed not with the X an unlettered man would make as his mark, but with a fine, flowing signature: *Dieter Karl Muller.* Herr Professor looked at it with satisfaction. "I see Mr. Muller has taken my advice. No need to wait until one knows how to read before learning to make a fine signature."

Karl's signature, as he signed below his father, was just as fine.

Chapter Fourteen

April 1849

Frau Alcott found the Mullers a place to live in what was called "half a house" out in Concord. The Alcotts had lived in the house once themselves, sharing it with the owners, who were friends. They were willing to let Frau Muller use the space for nothing in exchange for giving German lessons to their children. Concord was in the country, some twenty miles outside of Boston. The Mullers could go half of the way by train and would have to walk or take a wagon the rest of the way. Since they had no furniture to take with them, and only the clothes Frau Alcott had been able to round up for them, Mutti decided they would walk the last part of the journey. "The exercise will do us good," she said. She was glad to be going back to the country. May told Tilda and Hansi all about the glories of picnicking in the Concord woods and boating on the river, with Lotta acting as translator.

The Callaghans, too, had found a home, near relatives in the North End of Boston. Michael liked that. "I'm a city person. Sure an' I'd hate to be stuck out where th' rest o' youse is goin'."

Lotta was beginning to wonder if she wasn't a city person herself. No matter how much she'd hated it in the beginning, she felt at home here now. She hated the thought of starting over again. Especially when Vater would be sending for them before the year was out! Especially when it meant she wouldn't see the Alcotts any more, most of all Louy! She even began to wonder if she was going to like moving to Cincinnati.

Karl moved in with Gus and his family. Their last name was Thomson, and they'd been Market men for three generations. Gus's grandfather, an old man in his eighties, had seen the Battle of Bunker Hill in the American Revolution, and he told Karl war stories. Karl liked the Thomsons, and he particularly liked Mrs. Thomson's cooking. He began putting on airs about his own importance, and was so happy about his situation that Michael became quite envious. Gus promised to see if another Market man would take Michael on as an apprentice.

For Lotta, living with the Alcotts was sheer heaven. Yet slowly, as the days went by, she began to realize more and more that life was not sheer heaven for the Alcotts themselves. Kind Frau Alcott was always tired. She was out long hours, trying to help people in need, often without enough to give to fill those needs. Her temper was beginning to grow short. Herr Professor was also often out, and he didn't always come home when expected. Sometimes he walked for hours, to Concord and back, with no one knowing. He read a great deal, and wrote, but often Lotta would see him sitting motionless, his head on his hands. At those times his eyes were pained, or vague, or even dead. Louy saw this, too.

"He gets so discouraged," she confided to Louy. "It's worse in summer, somehow. He misses Mr. Emerson, out in Concord. If only I could make a school for him, or get his writing published! Maybe after I become famous, I can."

"But the 'conversations'? They go well?" Lotta ventured. Louy didn't answer.

They weren't bringing in money, at any rate, Lotta concluded. Food in the Alcott home was scarce, and she felt guilty about its being stretched to include her. She noticed that the Alcotts were taking in more sewing.

"Don't forget, those sheets aren't finished yet," Frau Alcott warned, when Louy came in jubilant about an order for two dozen hand-rolled handkerchiefs. "They're due this weekend."

"Yes, Marmee, I know," Louy murmured. But then, while embroidering, she was seized by inspiration and dashed for her manuscript and inkpot, and the sheets lay abandoned on the drawing-room sofa. By Saturday morning all but two monograms and two hems were completed. "I know, Marmee, I know," Louy said, as Frau Alcott was leaving on her endless errands.

By mid-morning Louy's eyes were aching. "Come take a run around the Common," she said to Lotta. "I need to get rid of the cobwebs!"

When they reached home again, Lizzie met them at the door. "Look what riches! Mrs. King had tickets for a musicale this afternoon and she can't use them. It's a matinee, so even May can go."

"Glory halleluia! How many tickets?" Louy cried, throwing her funny big-brimmed hat into the air.

"Three. Oh, I see . . . Lotta can have my ticket," Lizzie said quickly.

"Stuff and nonsense. If anyone stays home, it'll be May. She's the youngest."

"Nein. I stay home. You must all go," Lotta said, and would not be budged. By now she knew how much the quiet Lizzie loved music.

Shortly after lunch the three girls departed, dressed in their best. Herr Professor was out, so Lotta had the house to herself and she rather liked it. She was going to miss this so when she went to Cincinnati! She wandered through the quiet rooms, touching a book here, a polished tabletop there—

The sheets on which Louy had been sewing lay across the drawing-room sofa, unfinished. And they were due this evening.

Lotta knelt beside the sofa and looked at them. The embroi-
dery needle, its silk still in it, was thrust through the letter *M*.
The needlework was delicate, beautiful, the kind of stitchery
Mutti loved to do.

What a shame Mutti isn't here to complete it, Lotta thought. Frau
Alcott, even more than the sheets' owner, would be so grieved
if Louy did not complete the work on time. Then a second
thought struck her. Frau Alcott had admired *her* stitching. Louy
said she could earn money doing fine sewing—

Did she dare? *Could* she?

Louy had done so much for her.

Lotta washed her hands thoroughly. She rolled up her
sleeves and tied one of Frau Alcott's white aprons around her
neck and waist. Then she inspected Louy's workbasket. For
anyone as slapdash as Louy, it was remarkably neat, all the
little spools of thread and skeins of embroidery silk set out
carefully. There were papers of needles long and short, coarse
and fine.

At least I can finish the hemming, Lotta thought.

When she had completed it, only an hour and a half had
gone by. There were still the monograms . . .

Fortunately, the monograms had already been sketched on
the fabric by May in light blue pencil. It was only a matter of
satin-stitching over them, Lotta thought with relief. The work
was not as difficult as she had feared.

She was starting on the last sheet when the knocker sounded.
Michael stood there, grinning cheerfully. " 'Tis a foine day!
Come an' take a run round the Common, do!"

"I've already done that today," Lotta told him, laughing.

"Then do it agin! Too nice a day to be indoors!"

"I can't. I'm embroidering."

"Watcher doin' that fer? Silly waste o' time on a gorgeous
day, I'm thinkin'!"

"For money," Lotta said flatly. She didn't think it necessary
to add that the money would not be hers.

"Oh," Michael said. "That's different." He started to go.

"No! Wait!" Lotta heard her own voice saying. Michael turned back. "Could you—if you don't mind missing your run, you could deliver these for me when I'm finished? It won't be long. Maybe you'd get a coin or two for it," she added artfully. "I'm not promising, mind."

"I'll take the chance," Michael said quickly. He came inside and wandered around, inspecting Herr Professor's globe and pictures until the last monogram was done.

To Lotta's relief, the sheets could get by without pressing. She didn't trust herself to do that. Fortunately, Louy had pressed the hems in place before she'd started stitching. And they'd both been very careful with the monograms. What good luck, or good planning, that Louy had tucked a paper with the lady's name and address and the items ordered into her sewing basket! Lotta rummaged around until she found some paper to wrap the sheets in, pinned the wrappings shut, and tucked the paper in after repeating name and address twice to Michael. Like most people who read little, he had an excellent memory.

"Tell whoever answers that the package is from the Alcotts," she said. "And *be careful!*"

"Aye, aye, ma'am!" Michael saluted and marched off.

By now it was late afternoon. Lotta replaced the items in the sewing basket and closed it up. She took off the apron and put it away, and rolled down her sleeves. Herr Professor came in and sat down to read. As dusk was falling, Frau Alcott appeared. "Why, where are the girls?" she asked, looking around.

"A lady sent matinee tickets for them to use. For music."

"How kind," Frau Alcott said. "I hope—"

The door opened again. Louy, Lizzie, and May came in on a wave of enthusiasm. Lizzie was radiant. Louy turned a cartwheel in sheer delight. "Marmee, you should have been there! Mrs. King's an angel!"

"I'm glad you had the opportunity, and you must write and

thank her. You did finish the sheets before you went out, didn't you?" Frau Alcott asked.

Her back was turned, so she didn't see Louy's jaw drop in shock. Lotta spoke up quickly.

"Michael delivered them for her, Frau Alcott, just an hour ago."

"How nice. I'm proud of you, Louisa."

"Thank you, Marmee," Louy said in a low voice. Then they were caught up in the bustle of supper, but as soon as washing-up was over, Louy pulled Lotta into the bedroom.

"What happened?"

"Nothing. I finished the sheets for you, that's all. Michael came by looking for a walk, and I'd found the lady's address in your basket, so I had him deliver them." She repeated for Louy the instructions she'd given Michael.

"You're an angel straight from heaven, and I owe you more than I can repay," Louy said fervently. "You'll get the money for your work, of course."

"Of course *not!* It's little I can do, in return for all you've done for me," Lotta protested.

"I'll find a way to make it up to you, I promise," Louy said, and hugged her.

Chapter Fifteen

April 1849

Mutti was looking forward to the move to Concord. The thought of half a house, instead of one room, made her delirious. The thought of a country town, with a forest and a river, was intoxicating. She had written to Vater, and a letter in German, dictated by Vater to his employer's Swiss wife, had come back to Mutti. Vater was well, and content, and looking forward to their joining him. He was pleased with Karl's decision, and proud of all his children, although very disturbed about the fire. He sent his love to them all. "My first letter from my husband," Mutti said, misty-eyed, and put it in her trunk. Frau Alcott found a valise, shabby but sturdy, to hold the clothing she had gotten together for the Mullers. They could not go to Concord looking shiftless, even if they *were* refugees from a fire! More important, she had procured yards of fabric out of which Mutti could make new clothes for them all once they were in Concord.

"You will help with the sewing, *ja*, since you have become such a seamstress?" Mutti asked Lotta, as they packed the trunk the night before the move. To Mutti, and Mutti only, had Lotta confided the secret of the sheets.

When Lotta didn't answer, Mutti straightened and looked searchingly into her face. "Something is wrong, Daughter. What is it? Tell me."

"Mutti, I—" Lotta started over. "I don't want to go with you to Concord."

"*Was heisst?*" Mutti was genuinely startled.

"Mutti, please hear me out. I don't want to leave Boston. You'll be fine without me in Concord, and I can come to visit."

"*Liebchen*, you cannot stay in the city alone, a young girl! Where would you live?"

"With the Alcotts. Louy said I could stay with them as long as I wanted."

"And you are sure this is all right with Frau Alcott?"

"Louy wouldn't have said so if it weren't. Mutti, I love Boston. I'm learning so much from Louy, from all the Alcotts. I can help them with the sewing, and they say I'll be able to earn money as a seamstress soon."

"Two of my birds leaving the nest to earn their living." Mutti's eyes misted. "If you are sure, I will not stop you. Especially since we will be so near. You will come to me at end of summer. I have been told there is free school in Concord."

"Probably sooner. The Alcotts go away for part of the summer themselves. I'll write you, Mutti. Nearly every day. And I'll come visit."

Mutti and the children were leaving the next morning by an early train. The owner of the house would come by wagon to pick them up in Lexington. Frau Alcott had been anxious to get the Mullers settled into Concord before the Alcotts' own move, and Mutti was eager to be gone.

During that last week, Lotta had moved in with the Robinsons also, in order to help Mutti, and this last night before departure, Karl would spend there, too. "Don't tell the young ones about me yet," Lotta begged Mutti. "I'll tell Karl myself." When she did so, Karl looked at her with respect.

"Won't be so bad having you in the city," he said gruffly, but she understood.

They all rose at dawn, the Robinsons included, and Mr. Robinson and Karl loaded the two trunks into the wagon Mr. Robinson had arranged. Then Karl had to leave for the Market. Lotta was going to the train station with the family. They rattled off through the sun-streaked morning streets. At the station, Mr. Robinson unloaded the trunks and drove off. Lotta waited with the family for the train to come. At last the *putt-putt* of an engine, and the train's bell, sounded down the line.

"You're sure you won't come with us, *Liebchen?*" Mutti asked anxiously.

Lotta shook her head. "No country for me! Too many mosquitoes. Too many cows. I *like* the city! Besides," she added hastily, "it won't be long till Vater sends for us."

Lotta wasn't at all sure of this, for she had understood more of what Herr Professor had said than Mutti or Vater had. But she said it anyway, and Mutti smiled.

"*Ja*, we must remember that, and pray for him. And for Karl," Mutti said firmly.

Lotta nodded. Karl would need a lot of prayers—and more. He would need to hold his tongue. And to learn patience. *And so*, she thought ruefully, *do I*.

Mutti still looked anxious. "I don't like you staying in the city alone. It isn't safe."

"I won't be alone! I'll be with the Alcotts, remember? I'm going to work hard. And study—books, English, heaps of things! Maybe, when we are with Vater in Cincinnati, *I* can be a teacher! I'll make you proud, Mutti." Lotta hurried on as Mutti's eyes began to mist. "And—and when it gets too hot in Boston in the summer, I'll come stay with you in Concord."

Maybe, she added to herself.

The train pulled in, scattering sparks and covering everyone with cinders. People disembarked. An engineer loaded the Mullers' trunks aboard. Lotta stood on tiptoe to hug her

mother, Johannes and all, very hard. She kissed her brothers
and sisters, straightening their clothes, wiping dust and grime
off their faces. Trains gave off a lot of cinders!

A bell clanged noisily. The trainman shouted something they
couldn't understand and began rushing people onto the railroad
cars. Mutti and the children followed them. They found seats,
and Tilda and Hansi leaned out the window.

"*Auf Wiedersehen!*" they shouted.

Lotta smiled and waved as the train chugged out of the
station. "*Auf Wiedersehen!*" she shouted back.

When the train was a speck in the distance, she straightened
and settled her clothes properly. Already the day was growing
hot. Summer in Boston, Lotta remembered from last year, came
early. How much had happened since that day their ship pulled
into Boston harbor's Long Wharf! A lot she wanted to
forget . . . a lot she would remember forever.

"Maybe I'll write about some of it someday," Lotta thought.
"Or Louy will!"

She went back to the Robinsons, collected her shawl-
wrapped bundle, and gave Mrs. Robinson a grateful kiss goodbye. The Robinsons had been very kind, but they must be glad
to get their home back to themselves. They had taken the
Mullers in only because they understood what it was like to
be outsiders, and in need—and because they wanted to help
Frau Alcott. *As anybody but a* Dumkopf *would,* Lotta thought
fiercely, remembering some of the things she had seen and
heard over the past months.

She picked up her bundle and hurried off toward Dedham
Street, her heart singing. A whole new life was unrolling like
a scroll before her!

As she reached Louy's block, she saw Herr Professor on the
sidewalk before their lodging, and redoubled her speed despite
the heavy bundle. Then she froze.

Herr Professor was lifting Frau Alcott's rocker into a wagon
at the curb as two men hoisted Herr Professor's writing table.

Lizzie came up the steps carrying a lamp. Frau Alcott followed her with a blanket roll.

Lotta started to run. *"Herr Professor!"* she shouted.

Herr Professor straightened. A tall, thin figure in the wagon swung around and grinned. "Lotta! Hooray, you came to see us off!"

"Didn't you catch your train?" Herr Professor called anxiously.

"Mutti did—and the children—" Lotta gasped for breath. She stared imploringly at Louy. "I came—to stay with you—you *said* I could, anytime I want—"

Frau Alcott looked alarmed. "But child . . . you knew we were leaving here for the summer . . ."

"We're moving into the James Savage mansion for the summer," Abbie, perched on a trunk in the wagon, announced importantly. She flounced her skirts. "It's a very, very *elegant* residence."

"Abbie!" Annie and Frau Alcott cried automatically. Louy just stood staring at Lotta as though she knew exactly what was going through Lotta's mind.

To Lotta's shame, tears had rushed into her eyes. "But I thought . . . you said summer, and it's only May!"

"Our rent's paid till the first of June," Louy said. "But the Savages decided to leave for their summer vacation home early, so we can move now, too."

Lotta stared at her. "I thought you meant I could stay with you wherever you were. You said a girl could always earn money with her needle, and that there was more sewing here than you could do. I thought maybe . . . when summer does come . . ."

She couldn't finish.

Frau Alcott set down her blanket roll and put her arms around Lotta. "I wish we could take you with us, but you see, it is a friend's home, and we mustn't presume upon his kindness. He and his wife have done so much for us already. You were meant to go with your mother, child. You knew that. We bought you a train ticket."

Lotta brought it out of her pocket. "I thought I could use it later . . . after I'd earned some money to bring to Mutti . . ."

Herr Professor and his wife exchanged glances. "Perhaps Mrs. Robinson would keep her a bit longer," Frau Alcott said.

"Christopher Columbus!" Louy jumped down from the wagon, her eyes sparking. "Don't you see the girl feels bad enough already! You can't just pass her around like a sack of potatoes!"

She put her hands on Lotta's shoulders and marched her away to where Herr Professor and Frau Alcott couldn't overhear. "Now, listen! You'll have to go to your mother today, that's all there is to it. But soon as you've settled, and cleaned yourself up a bit—" Her eyes twinkled, taking in Lotta's soot-streaked face. She fished in her pocket and came up with some coins. "I was saving this for Mr. Dickens' new book, but you can have it for carfare. Mother doesn't know this, but I've spoken to our cousins and the lady who ordered the sheets about you. She needs someone to do fine sewing, and she may let you live in, if you present yourself properly. Not putting on airs or telling fibs, mind you . . . just conducting yourself like a young woman old enough to work on her own."

Lotta gasped. "But I can't—"

Louy's face grew stern. "Do you or do you not want to help your family? Did you or did you not tell me you were bound and determined to pull yourself up? That you'd do whatever it took, any honest work, to do so? Or do you still expect the streets of America to be paved with gold for the taking . . . or other folks to shower it on you just because of your high-minded ideals and good intentions? Christopher Columbus, hasn't *anything* you've seen and heard this winter sunk in?"

Lotta felt as if every inch of her skin were burning. "I *don't* expect—! I didn't mean—!" She willed her jaw to stop

143

trembling and stared at Louy with every ounce of pride she possessed. "I'm sorry. I won't bother you again."

"Now you're going overboard in the opposite direction! Sakes alive, Carlotta, why in tarnation do you have to take after my worst traits as well as my best?" Louy's eyes softened, and she lowered her voice. "Now, listen. Thanks to the Savages, Father and Marmee will live in luxury for the summer. With all that's happened the past year or so, Marmee's had more than she can take, physically and otherwise. And I'm really worried about Father's state of mind. That's why it's so good for us to move this early. I mean Marmee to have a quiet summer, not worrying about anything or anybody. That's why you can't live with us. It would remind her of all the endless needs in this blessed city that even her hard work and best intentions can't fill. And Father—"

To her astonishment, Lotta saw naked fear in Louy's eyes. "Father's given, and *given*, and folks don't appreciate and won't understand . . . any more than he'll understand how impracti-cal—" As if conscious of disloyalty, Louy cut herself off and took a deep breath. "You've been good for Father, do you know that, Lotta?"

Lotta's jaw dropped. "Me? For Herr Professor?"

"*Ja, Liebchen*. And if you're grateful, you'll remember how much he sees in you, and *use* it. Remember his stories." Her eyes glinted. "And you might be grateful to me for getting you an opportunity to be a *real* seamstress!"

Lotta looked at her blankly. "*Was bedeutch* seamstress?" she asked, slipping back into German.

"Didn't you hear a word I said? I confessed to our distant cousin who'd *really* made her sheets. She was very pleased. She was interested in having you sew for her during the summer. I told her you were leaving this morning, but since you're still here, you can call on her. Maybe she'll give you work to take with you to Concord."

Lotta stared at Louy in a mixture of joy and fear. "I can't call on a grand lady I don't know and ask for work!"

"Of *course* you can! Wait a minute." Louy stalked over to her mother and spoke to her in an undertone. Frau Alcott turned to look at Lotta with surprise and pleasure.

"The very thing! I'm proud of Louy for thinking of it . . . and ashamed of myself for not thinking of it first. Lotta, I'm sure the Robinsons will let you stay with them for another night or so. You must go to Mrs. Robinson right now, explain the reason, and ask her nicely."

"I will," Lotta promised, her fingers crossed.

"Then call on my cousin on Pickney Street," Frau Alcott urged. "Tell her I said it would be possible for you to do sewing for her, if she so wishes, while you are in Concord with your mother. If you please her with your manner, and manners, as well as your needlework, your career as a needlewoman will be launched. Indeed, she would probably let you live in while sewing, if you had your mother's blessing. But of course, as things are arranged now, that wouldn't do."

Another idea, scary and exciting, began rioting in Lotta's brain. She dropped her eyes demurely so it wouldn't show, but not before catching Louy's glance of wicked understanding. Louy grinned.

"Goodbye for now, fellow pilgrim," she hissed conspiratorially. "Don't do anything I wouldn't do. And don't do anything I *would* do and shouldn't! And *write!* In your journal. And to me, you hear?" She shook hands with Lotta, then hugged her hard.

Frau Alcott bent and kissed Lotta. "God bless you, child. Don't disappoint me, now!"

"I won't," Lotta promised.

"And give my love to your mother."

"Yes, ma'am," Lotta said demurely.

Herr Professor put his hand on Lotta's head and wished her well. "Mrs. Alcott and I each have a little gift for you. We intended to mail them to you in Concord, but since you're here, you can take them with you. They will be a help to you this summer, and a guide in your new life in the West." He pressed two small packages into her hand. Annie and Lizzie also handed her packages. They each hugged her, and so, to Lotta's surprise, did May.

"You're really quite pretty when your face isn't sour," May said kindly. "I have something for you, too. It's my second-best ribbon. It's only a little scorched. That was Louy's fault, and if you're careful when you tie it, the scorch won't show. Remember to plaster it against a looking-glass to dry when you wash it." She skipped off to climb into the wagon next to Lizzie.

Lotta stood waving after them until the wagon turned out of sight at the end of Dedham Street. Then she took a deep breath and turned, not toward the Robinsons, but toward the house behind her. The Alcotts had not locked it; she had watched to be sure. She pushed the door open cautiously and stepped inside.

The bookshelves were empty in the drawing room, but the couch still stood there. She had thought it would be, since it hadn't been on the wagon. The beds were stripped and bare, but still in place. So was the little table in the kitchen, though dishes, pots, and pans were gone. Lotta smiled to herself. She could live here quite well, if she had to. If she was careful.

Maybe she wouldn't have to.

Maybe she could start a Muller Sinking Fund before Vater sent for them to come to Cincinnati.

If she had the courage.

Lotta looked around. The bathtub was gone, but there was still a large tub for heating water. She pumped some and set the tub on the stove, which she lit carefully with matches found in a kitchen cupboard. Then she locked the door and pulled down all the shades. She sat on the sofa and opened the Alcotts' packages, one by one.

The first two were books. One was a brown-bound volume

of *Pilgrim's Progress* with *To a good little pilgrim, from Amos Bronson Alcott* written inside. Frau Alcott had given her a small New Testament bound in a pale blue leather, with a loving message inside along with a list of verses she should read. Frau Alcott had written out a quotation from Hebrews:

> *Now faith is the substance of things hoped for, the*
> *evidence of things not seen . . .*
> *By faith Abraham, when he was called to go into a place*
> *which he should afterward receive as an inheritance, obeyed;*
> *and he went out, not knowing whither he went . . .*
> *. . . they were strangers and pilgrims on the earth.*

Annie had given her a set of white collar and cuffs, edged with her own fine crocheting. Lizzie's parcel contained one of her own dresses, a dark navy blue. Lotta held it up. It came down to her ankles, which would make her look at least two years older! The strangely shaped and wrapped parcel Louy had thrust on her at the last moment contained a bonnet—an actual, fine American lady straw bonnet. *Specially assembled and trimmed for Fraulein Carlotta Muller by Sairy Gamp,* read the card, in Louy's slanting script. Sairy Gamp was a character Louy adored from one of Mr. Dickens' books.

When the water was not quite boiling, Lotta took it off the stove and scrubbed herself all over. She put on the underthings she had made, under Frau Alcott's guidance, for her trip to the West. No need for the flannel under-petticoat in summer, but the chemise, the knee-length drawers that buttoned onto it, the plain muslin under-petticoat, and the outer-petticoat trimmed with fine tucking and narrow crochet went on in turn. Then the cotton stockings, rolled neatly just below the knees. She polished the handed-down-from-Annie boots with spit until they gleamed. Then she put on the dress, which fitted perfectly and was satisfyingly long. The collar and cuffs were

147

just right with it, and Annie had thoughtfully provided the necessary pins.

Lotta braided her hair—loosely, as May had said was more becoming—and, in Mutti's absence, looped it up. The effect, when Lotta stood on tiptoe to peer into the glass, was startling.

"I look almost as old as Louy!" she breathed.

Now the bonnet. She lifted it, set it on carefully . . .

The transformation was complete.

Before she could get the shakes and lose her nerve, Lotta went out the front door and locked it firmly behind her. She unbuttoned her bodice at the breast, tucked the key inside her chemise, and buttoned herself up again. The key was safe, its cord wound carefully around one of the chemise's buttons.

She headed toward the Common.

The dome of the State House sparkled with gold in the morning sun, and everywhere flowers were in bloom. Children were rolling hoops around the footpaths. Brisk maids were sweeping front steps, and horses trotted smartly past, drawing delivery wagons or the gentry's buggies.

Her eyes on the ground so she wouldn't trip or fall, Lotta started across the Common, reciting the address and her prepared speech over and over beneath her breath so she would not forget.

On Pinckney Street sunlight gilded brass knockers and doorknobs, and birds were singing in the trees. She reached the house. She took a deep breath, said a quick prayer, and marched up the steps.

The knocker gave an elegant *clank*. Lotta's heart hammered as she waited. Before she could lose her nerve and flee, the door opened and a trim maid stood there.

"Fraulein Carlotta Muller calling, on Mrs. Alcott's direction," Lotta announced, in a voice admirably free of quavers.

The maid didn't send her off. The maid didn't look at her as though she were a dirty foreigner. The maid said, "Will you wait, please, Miss? I'll see if Madam can receive you."

Lotta waited, holding her breath.

After several minutes a pretty, middle-aged woman in an exquisite morning dress of lace-trimmed flowered silk appeared. "You wished to see me?" she asked, smiling.

Lotta took a deep breath and smiled back, not enough to seem forward, just enough to be polite. "Good morning, Madam. I am Fraulein Carlotta Muller. My friend Louisa May Alcott told me you were interested in having me do fine sewing for you. I can live in, if desired."

"Oh, yes. Come in." Lotta followed. Her new life in America had begun.

Author's Note

This book, *Lotta's Progress*, is fiction. I have made up the Mullers and the Callaghans out of my imagination and research, though many families like them came to the United States between 1840 and 1917, looking for a better life. The Alcotts, on the other hand, are very real. The idea for this story came to me out of my researching and writing *Louisa May: The World and Works of Louisa May Alcott.* "Herr Professor" is Amos Bronson Alcott, a Transcendentalist philosopher and pioneer educator so far ahead of his time that educational theory only recently began catching up with him. "Frau Alcott" is Abigail May Alcott, one of the first, if not *the* first, professional social workers. "Louy" was the childhood nickname of Louisa May Alcott, who with her book *Little Women* and its sequels became the first author of what are now known as young adult novels—realistic portrayals of teenage life. (In her own lifetime, incidentally, they were bestsellers for adult readers as well!) "Annie," "Louy," "Lizzie," and "May"—Anna Bronson Alcott Pratt, Louisa May Alcott, Elizabeth Sewall Alcott, and Abbie May Alcott Nieriker—are beloved by readers everywhere as the characters Meg, Jo, Beth, and Amy March.

The things that happened to the Alcotts in *Lotta's Progress* actually happened to them in real life. The Dedham Street, Boston, house was where they actually lived between autumn 1848 and spring 1849, and they did then move into Mr. and Mrs. James Savage's home for the summer. Their activities in this book, and the ideas they express, are accurate. So are portrayals of the friends and relatives they speak of. The Robinson family was also real. The stories Louy is writing in this book have all been published; the plays she talks about Louisa actually wrote.

We know that Louisa May Alcott based characters and events in her young adult novels on actual people and events, most of them within her own family. Many passages in the March novels she copied almost word for word out of her own letters and journals. So in creating the fictional stories of the Mullers and the Callaghans, I have been guided by clues in Louisa's own stories, as well as in her mother's unpublished journals and social work reports. I asked myself, "What people could Louisa have known who might have been models for those characters in her stories? What might have happened to them that suggested such-and-such plot incidents to her?" A family much like the Mullers must have been the model for the Hummels in *Little Women*. Readers can have their own fun trying to figure out what other incidents in *Lotta's Progress* match up with incidents in Louisa's own novels, and they can read biographies of the Alcott family to find out which match up with real life.

—Norma Johnston

Recipes Mentioned in *Lotta's Progress*

Scripture Cake

3 firm *baking apples*
¼ tsp. *ground cinnamon*
½ tsp. *granulated sugar*
4 cups *all-purpose flour*
1 tsp. *baking soda*
1 tsp. *more ground cinnamon*
½ tsp. *ground cloves*
¼ tsp. *ground ginger*
6 *eggs*
1 cup *buttermilk (or substitute regular milk)*

⅔ cup *honey*
1 cup (2 sticks) *butter*
1½ cups *molasses*
1½ cups *raisins*
1½ cups *chopped dried figs*
1 cup *slivered almonds*
Orange juice (optional)

Measure all ingredients before beginning. Grease and flour (or line with foil and grease) 2 pans—9 × 5 × 3" loaf pans or 9" square pans.

Peel and core apples and cut into 8 sections. Cut each section into 4 to 6 pieces. Sprinkle lightly with ¼ tsp. ground cinnamon and the granulated sugar and set aside.

In a medium-sized bowl, combine flour, baking soda, cinnamon, cloves, and ginger. Beat eggs in medium-sized bowl, then beat in buttermilk and honey. Cream butter till fluffy in a large bowl, then add molasses and stir well.

Add about ⅓ of flour mixture to creamed butter and mix well. Add about ⅓ of egg mixture to creamed butter and mix well. Repeat twice, so that all flour and egg mixtures have been added.

Add raisins, figs, and almonds, and stir well.

Lightly fold in apple pieces.

Turn mixture into prepared pans. Bake loaf pans at 325° F for 40 minutes *or* square pans for 30 minutes.

Cover loosely with foil. Bake loaf pans for 50 minutes more *or* square pans for 40 minutes more.

152

Remove from oven and let cool in pans 10 minutes. Brush tops with orange juice, if desired.

Notes

To make only one cake, cut recipe in half.
This cake freezes well.

Apple Cake

2 cups sifted all-purpose flour
½ cup granulated sugar
2½ tsp. baking powder
pinch of salt
1 egg
1 cup milk or half-and-half
½ tsp. vanilla

⅓ cup butter, melted and cooled,
  or ⅓ cup vegetable oil
2 firm baking apples, peeled,
  cored, and cut into small
  chunks
granulated sugar or brown sugar
  (optional)

Grease and flour, or line with foil and grease, an 8" or 9" square or round baking pan, 1" to 2" deep.

Combine flour, sugar, baking powder, and salt in a large bowl. Beat egg in milk or cream, stir in melted butter or oil and vanilla, and add to dry ingredients. Stir *only until flour is moistened*. Batter will be lumpy.

Fold approximately 1 cup of apple chunks into batter. Pour batter into prepared pan.

Bake in 400° F oven until a skewer or cake tester inserted comes out clean—about 18 to 22 minutes. Sprinkle top with granulated sugar or brown sugar, if desired.

Notes

Vanilla ice cream goes well with this recipe.
This cake freezes well.

Split-Pea Soup

1 lb. dried green split peas
5 cups beef or vegetable broth
   or plain water (bouillon
   cubes dissolved in water can
   be used)
1 large onion, chopped
1 cup celery, chopped (optional)
2 large or 3 medium carrots,
   peeled and chopped

2 medium garlic cloves, chopped
1 tsp. dried thyme leaves
½ tsp. dried marjoram leaves
¼ tsp. coarse-ground black
   pepper
salt to taste

Spread dried peas out, about ¼ packet at a time, on a large plate or tray. Discard any that look like dark pebbles.

Put peas into a large strainer (a few at a time is easiest) and rinse under cold running water. Transfer peas to a large, heavy soup pot *or* a large casserole that can be used over a stove burner. (An enamel cast-iron casserole is ideal.)

In another pot, bring soup liquid (broth, bouillon or water) to a boil. Pour boiling liquid over peas, cover, and allow to stand for 1 hour to soften peas and until water cools.

After an hour, turn heat to *high* under peas, bring to a boil, and *immediately* reduce heat to low. Cook, barely boiling, over low heat for a ½ hour, stirring frequently.

Add remaining ingredients and cook over low heat, stirring frequently, until peas are soft enough to be squashed by your stirring spoon and other vegetables are soft. If mixture becomes too thick to eat as soup, add water *immediately*, about ¼ cup at a time, stirring constantly.

Push soup, a cup at a time, through a coarse strainer into another pot (or puree in a blender and return to another pot). Bring soup to boil, remove from heat, and serve.

Notes

This soup burns very easily, especially when cooked on an electric stove. You must watch it constantly and stir frequently.

While cooking, partially cover pot with a lid. An uncovered, or totally covered, pot can result in a pea-green kitchen ceiling.

Thin slices of frankfurter or sausage, or slivers of cooked ham, can be added during the final cooking.

Croutons and/or crumbled, cooked bacon can be sprinkled on top.

This soup can be made, in small batches, in a microwave oven.